LAUGH
OUT
LOUD

A selection of the finest internet humour, anecdotes and wisdom

Vivienne Smithdorf   Vanessa Wilson

VSQUARED
PUBLISHING

© Vsquared Publishing cc 2004

First published 2004

ISBN 0-620-32050-8

Published by Vsquared Publishing cc
PO Box 786582 Sandton 2146 South Africa
info@publisher.co.za
www.publisher.co.za

Designed and typeset by Vanessa Wilson
Edited by Rachel Bey-Miller
Printed and bound by Creda Communications (Pty) Ltd, Epping II

The views expressed in this book are not necessarily those of the publisher or its employees.

Contents

Children, Parenting and Pets 5

Business and Technology 27

Relationships and the Sexes 83

Ageing and Health 113

Language and Academics 133

Life, Wisdom and Motivation 165

Everything Else 181

Acknowledgements

We would like to thank Rachel Bey-Miller for her advice and editing assistance; Susie and Barry Smithdorf for reading the manuscript and providing valuable feedback; and other friends who were willing springboards for our ideas. Our heartfelt appreciation goes especially to all those friends and acquaintances who, through years of kind and tireless e-mail forwarding of jokes and interesting bits and pieces, effectively created the heart of the book. And, of course, our sincere thanks to all who penned the contents of the pages that follow: both to those who generously granted us permission to reprint their pieces and also to those original authors who we were regrettably unable to trace. You have all helped make this book possible.

Children, Parenting and Pets

Parents of teenagers know why animals eat their young.

How to know whether you are ready for kids

✓ **Mess test**

Smear peanut butter on the sofa and curtains. Place a fish stick behind the couch and leave it there all summer.

✓ **Toy test**

Obtain a 55-litre box of Lego (you may substitute roofing tacks). Have a friend spread them all over the house. Put on a blindfold. Try to walk to the bathroom or kitchen. Do not scream because this would wake a child at night.

✓ **Grocery store test**

Borrow one or two small animals (goats are best) and take them with you as you shop. Always keep them in sight and pay for anything they eat or damage.

✓ **Dressing test**

Obtain one large, unhappy, live octopus. Stuff into a small net bag making sure that all the arms stay inside.

✓ **Feeding test**

Obtain a large plastic milk jug. Fill halfway with water. Suspend from the ceiling with a cord. Start the jug swinging. Try to insert spoonfuls of soggy cereal into the mouth of the jug, while pretending to be an airplane. Now dump the contents of the jug on the floor.

✓ **Night test**

Prepare by obtaining a small cloth bag and fill it with 4–5 kg of sand. Soak it thoroughly in water. At 3 pm begin to waltz and hum with the bag until 9 pm. Lay down your bag and set your alarm for 10 pm. Get up, pick up your bag, and sing every song you have ever heard. Make up about a dozen more and sing these too until 4 am. Set alarm for 5 am. Get up and make breakfast. Keep this up for 5 years. Look cheerful.

✓ Ingenuity test

Take an egg carton. Using a pair of scissors and a pot of paint, turn it into an alligator. Now take a toilet paper tube and turn it into an attractive Christmas candle. Use only scotch tape and a piece of foil. Lastly, take a milk carton, a ping-pong ball, and an empty box of Cocoa Puffs. Make an exact replica of the Eiffel Tower.

✓ Automobile test

Forget the BMW and buy a station wagon. Buy a chocolate ice cream cone and put it in the glove compartment. Leave it there. Get a dime. Stick it into the cassette player. Take a family size package of chocolate chip cookies. Mash them into the back seat. Run a garden rake along both sides of the car. There, perfect.

✓ Physical test (women)

Obtain a large bean bag chair and attach it to the front of your clothes. Leave it there for 9 months. Now remove 10 of the beans. Try not to notice your closet full of clothes. You won't be wearing them for a while.

✓ Physical test (men)

Go to the nearest pharmacy. Set your wallet on the counter. Ask the clerk to help himself. Now proceed to the nearest food store. Go to the head office and arrange for your paycheck to be directly deposited to the store. Purchase a newspaper. Go home and read it quietly for the last time.

✓ Final assignment

Find a couple who already have a small child. Lecture them on how they can improve their discipline, patience, tolerance, toilet training and child's table manners. Emphasize to them that they should never allow their children to run wild. Enjoy this experience. It will be the last time you will have all the answers.

•••

Baby perspectives

Your Clothes

1st baby – You begin wearing maternity clothes as soon as your ob-gyn confirms your pregnancy.

2nd baby – You wear your regular clothes for as long as possible.

3rd baby – Your regular clothes are your maternity clothes.

The Baby's Name

1st baby – You pore over baby-name books and practise pronouncing and writing combinations of all your favourites.

2nd baby – Someone has to name their kid after your great-aunt Mavis, right? It might as well be you.

3rd baby – You open a name book, close your eyes, and see where your finger falls. Bimaldo? Perfect!

Preparing for the Birth

1st baby – You practise your breathing regularly.

2nd baby – You don't bother practising because you remember that, last time, breathing didn't do a thing.

3rd baby – You ask for an epidural in the eighth month.

The Layette

1st baby – You pre-wash your newborn's clothes, colour-coordinate them, and fold them neatly in the baby's little bureau.

2nd baby – You check to make sure that the clothes are clean and discard only the ones with the darkest stains.

3rd baby – Boys can wear pink, can't they?

Worries

1st baby – At the first sign of distress – a whimper, a frown – you pick up the baby.

2nd baby – You pick up the baby when her wails threaten to wake your firstborn.

3rd baby – You teach your three-year-old how to rewind the mechanical swing.

Activities

1st baby – You take your infant to Baby Gymnastics, Baby Swing, and Baby Story Hour.

2nd baby – You take your infant to Baby Gymnastics.

3rd baby – You take your infant to the supermarket and the dry cleaners.

Going Out

1st baby – The first time you leave your baby with a sitter, you call home five times.

2nd baby – Just before you walk out the door, you remember to leave a number where you can be reached.

3rd baby – You leave instructions for the sitter to call only if she sees blood.

At Home

1st baby – You spend a good bit of every day just gazing at the baby.

2nd baby – You spend a bit of every day watching to be sure your older child isn't squeezing, poking, or hitting the baby.

3rd baby – You spend a little bit of every day hiding from the children.

– Appeared in February 1998 issue of *Parenting*

• • •

A three-year-old boy went with his dad to see a litter of kittens. On returning home, he breathlessly informed his mother, "There were two boy kittens and two girl kittens." "How did you know?" his mother asked. "Daddy picked them up and looked underneath," he replied. "I think it's printed on the bottom."

• • •

Another three-year-old put his shoes on by himself. His mother noticed the left was on the right foot. She said, "Son, your shoes are on the wrong feet." He looked up at her with a raised brow and said, "Don't kid me, Mom. I KNOW they're my feet."

• • •

Pregnancy and women

Q: Should I have a baby after 35?
A: No, 35 children is enough.

Q: I'm two months pregnant now. When will my baby move?
A: With any luck, right after he finishes college.

Q: What is the most reliable method to determine a baby's sex?
A: Childbirth.

Q: My wife is five months pregnant and so moody that sometimes she's borderline irrational.
A: So what's your question?

Q: My childbirth instructor says it's not pain I'll feel during labour, but pressure. Is she right?
A: Yes, in the same way that a tornado might be called an air current.

Q: When is the best time to get an epidural?
A: Right after you find out you're pregnant.

Q: Is there any reason I have to be in the delivery room while my wife is in labour?
A: Not unless the word 'alimony' means anything to you.

Q: Our baby was born last week. When will my wife begin to feel and act normal again?
A: When your child leaves home.

• • •

A father was reading Bible stories to his young son. He read, "The man named Lot was warned to take his wife and flee out of the city but his wife looked back and was turned to salt." His son asked, "What happened to the flea?"

• • •

My friend likes to read his two young sons fairy tales at night. Having a deep-rooted sense of humour, he often ad-libs parts of the stories for fun.

One day, his youngest son was sitting in his first grade class as the teacher was reading the story of the Three Little Pigs.

She came to the part of the story where the first pig was trying to acquire building materials for his home. She said, "... and so the pig went up to the man with a wheelbarrow full of straw and said 'Pardon me sir, but might I have some of that straw to build my house?'"

Then the teacher asked the class, "And what do you think that man said?" My friend's son raised his hand and said, "I know! I know! 'Holy smoke! A talking pig!'"

•••

Describe a bird or an animal

Here is a delightful essay written by a 10-year-old which appeared in a 1945 newspaper:

"The bird I am going to write about is the owl. The owl cannot see by day, and at night is blind as a bat. I do not know much about the owl so I will go on to the beast which I am going to choose.

It is the cow. The cow is a mammal. It has six sides – right, left, an upper and below. At the back it has a tail on which hangs a brush. With this it sends the flies away so they do not fall into the milk.

The head is for the purpose of growing horns and so that the mouth can be somewhere. The horns are to butt with and the mouth is to moo with.

Under the cow hangs the milk. It is arranged for milking. When people milk, the milk comes and there is no end to the supply. How the cow does it I have not yet realized, but it makes more and more.

The cow has a fine sense of smell. One can smell it far away. This is the reason for the fresh air in the country.

The male cow is called an ox. It is not a mammal. The cow doesn't eat much, but what it eats it eats twice so that it gets enough. When it is hungry it moos, and when it says nothing it is because its inside is all full up with grass."

• • •

Those well-known proverbs

Some 6-year-olds were given well-known proverbs to complete. This is what they came up with ...

▶ Better to be safe than ... punch a Grade 7 boy.
▶ Strike while the ... insect is close.
▶ It's always darkest before ... Daylight Saving Time.
▶ Never underestimate the power of ... ants.
▶ You can lead a horse to water but ... how?
▶ Don't bite the hand that ... looks dirty.
▶ No news is ... impossible.
▶ A miss is as good as a ... Mr.
▶ You can't teach an old dog new ... maths.
▶ If you lie down with dogs, you'll ... stink in the morning.
▶ Love all, trust ... me.
▶ The pen is mightier than the ... pigs.
▶ An idle mind is ... the best way to relax.
▶ Where there's smoke there's ... pollution.
▶ Happy the bride who ... gets all the presents.
▶ A penny saved is ... not much.
▶ Two's company, three's ... the Musketeers.
▶ Don't put off till tomorrow what ... you put on to go to bed.
▶ Laugh and the whole world laughs with you, cry and ... you have to blow your nose.
▶ There are none so blind as ... Stevie Wonder.
▶ Children should be seen and not ... smacked or grounded.
▶ If at first you don't succeed ... get new batteries.
▶ You get out of something only what you ... see in the picture on the box.
▶ When the blind leadeth the blind ... get out of the way.

• • •

Quotes from children's science answers

▶ Water is composed of two gins, Oxygin and Hydrogin. Oxygin is pure gin. Hydrogin is gin and water.

▶ When you breathe, you inspire. When you do not breathe, you expire.

▶ H2O is hot water, and CO2 is cold water.

▶ Three kinds of blood vessels are arteries, vanes, and caterpillars.

▶ Blood flows down one leg and up the other.

▶ The moon is a planet just like the earth, only it is even deader.

▶ A super-saturated solution is one that holds more than it can hold.

▶ Mushrooms always grow in damp places and so they look like umbrellas.

▶ The body consists of three parts – the brainium, the borax and the abominable cavity. The brainium contains the brain, the borax contains the heart and lungs, and the abominable cavity contains the bowels, of which there are five – a, e, i, o and u.

▶ Before giving a blood transfusion, find out if the blood is affirmative or negative.

▶ To remove dust from the eye, pull the eye down over the nose.

▶ For a nosebleed: put the nose much lower than the body until the heart stops.

▶ For fainting: rub the person's chest or, if a lady, rub her arm above the hand instead.

▶ For a dog bite: put the dog away for several days. If he has not recovered, then kill it.

▶ For asphyxiation: apply artificial respiration until the patient is dead.

▶ For a head cold: use an agonizer to spray the nose until it drops in your throat.

▶ The pistol of a flower is its only protection against insects.

▶ The skeleton is what is left after the insides have been taken out and the outsides have been taken off. The purpose of the skeleton is something to hitch meat to.

▸ The alimentary canal is located in the northern part of Indiana.
▸ The tides are a fight between the Earth and moon. All water tends towards the moon, because there is no water in the moon, and nature abhors a vacuum. I forget where the sun joins in the fight.
▸ A fossil is an extinct animal. The older it is, the more extinct it is.
▸ Momentum: what you give a person when they are going away
▸ Planet: a body of earth surrounded by sky
▸ Rhubarb: a kind of celery gone bloodshot
▸ Vacuum: a large, empty space where the Pope lives
▸ Equator: a managerie lion running around the Earth through Africa
▸ Germinate: to become a naturalized German
▸ Litter: a nest of young puppies
▸ Magnet: something you find crawling all over a dead cat

What my mother taught me

▸ My mother taught me to APPRECIATE A JOB WELL DONE: "If you're going to kill each other, do it outside – I've just finished cleaning!"
▸ My mother taught me RELIGION: "You'd better pray that comes out of the carpet."
▸ My mother taught me LOGIC: "If you fall out of that swing and break your neck, you're not going to the store with me."
▸ My mother taught me IRONY: "Keep crying and I'll give you something to cry about."
▸ My mother taught me about the science of OSMOSIS: "Shut your mouth and eat your supper!"
▸ My mother taught me about THE CIRCLE OF LIFE: "I brought you into this world, and I can take you out."
▸ My mother taught me HUMOUR: "When that lawnmower cuts off your toes, don't come running to me."

•••

The crocodile

This is a real exam of a Grade 5 primary school pupil.

Q: Write an essay on the following question: "What is a crocodile?" Use block letters and write legibly.

A: Name: John Smith
Date: Monday 22/05/2000

"The crokodile is specially built so long because the flatter the better swimmer. At the front of the crocodile is the head. The head exists almost only of teeth. Behind the crocodile the tail grows.

Between the head and the tail is the crocodile. A crocodile without a tail is called a rotwieler. A crocodile's body is covered with handbag material. He can throw his tail off if he gets a fright but it doesn't happen much because a crocodile is scared of nothing.

A crocodile stays under the water because if you were so ugly, you would also stay under the water. It is good that a crocodile stays under the water, because a person gets such a big fright if a crocodile catches you that he first has to rinse you off before he can eat you.

A crocodile isn't hardly as dangerous as people say he is, except if he catches you. The longer he bites you, the more it hurts. Very old crocodiles suck their people and buck that they catch dead. If you eat him, he is a crocosatie.

A crocodile did not learn to swim with his arms so he uses his tail. The little brother of the crocodile is a lizard. The slow sister of the crocodile is a chameleon. The gay brother of the crocodile is a daffodil. And the crocodile also has a dead brother the frikkidel!"

• • •

On the first day of school, the Kindergarten teacher said, "If anyone has to go to the bathroom, hold up two fingers." A little voice from the back of the room asked, "How will that help?"

• • •

Bright answers to questions on dating and marriage

How do you decide who to marry?

You got to find somebody who likes the same stuff. Like, if you like sports, she should like it that you like sports, and she should keep the chips and dip coming. – *Alan, age 10*

No person really decides before they grow up who they're going to marry. God decides it all way before, and you get to find out later who you're stuck with. – *Kirsten, age 10*

What is the right age to get married?

Twenty-three is the best age because you know the person FOREVER by then. – *Camille, age 10*

No age is good to get married at. You got to be a fool to get married.
– *Freddie, age 6*

How can a stranger tell if two people are married?

You might have to guess, based on whether they seem to be yelling at the same kids. – *Derrick, age 8*

Is it better to be single or married?

It's better for girls to be single but not for boys. Boys need someone to clean up after them. – *Anita, age 9*

What do most people do on a date?

Dates are for having fun, and people should use them to get to know each other. Even boys have something to say if you listen long enough.
– *Lynnette, age 8*

On the first date, they just tell each other lies, and that usually gets them interested enough to go for a second date.
– *Martin, age 10*

What would you do on a first date that was turning sour?

I'd run home and play dead. The next day I would call all the newspapers and make sure they wrote about me in all the dead columns.
– *Craig, age 9*

When is it okay to kiss someone?

When they're rich. – *Pam, age 7*

The law says you have to be eighteen, so I wouldn't want to mess with that. – *Curt, age 7*

The rule goes like this: If you kiss someone, then you should marry them and have kids with them. It's the right thing to do.
– *Howard, age 8*

How would you make a marriage work?

Tell your wife that she looks pretty even if she looks like a truck.
– *Ricky, age 10*

•••

The children had all been photographed, and the teacher was trying to persuade them each to buy a copy of the group picture. "Just think how nice it will be to look at it when you are all grown up and say, 'There's Emily; she's a lawyer,' or 'That's David; he's a doctor.'"

A small voice at the back of the room rang out, "And there's the teacher ... she's dead."

•••

One summer evening during a violent thunderstorm a mother was tucking her small boy into bed. She was about to turn off the light when he asked with a tremor in his voice, "Mommy, will you sleep with me tonight?"

The mother smiled and gave him a reassuring hug. "I can't, dear," she said. "I have to sleep with Daddy."

A long silence was broken at last by his shaky little voice: "The big sissy."

Mom's Dictionary

Amnesia: A condition that enables a woman who has gone through labour to consider having children again.

Dumb waiter: One who asks if the kids would care to order dessert.

Family planning: The art of spacing your children the proper distance apart to keep you on the edge of financial disaster.

Feedback: The inevitable result when your baby doesn't appreciate the strained carrots.

Full name: What you call your child when you're mad at him.

Grandparents: The people who think your children are wonderful even though they're sure you're not raising them correctly.

Hearsay: What toddlers do when anyone mutters a dirty word.

Impregnable: A woman whose memory of labour is still vivid.

Independent: How we want our children to be as long as they do everything we say.

Ow: The first word spoken by children with older siblings.

Show off: A child who is more talented than yours.

Sterilize: What you do to your first baby's pacifier by boiling it and to your last baby's pacifier by blowing on it.

Top bunk: Where you should never put a child wearing Superman pajamas.

Two minute warning: When the baby's face turns red and she begins to make those familiar grunting noises.

Verbal: able to whine in words.

Whodunit: None of the kids that live in your house.

•••

> If I want to hear the pitter patter of little feet,
> I'll put shoes on my cat.

More children's science answers

Q: Name the four seasons.
A: Salt, pepper, mustard and vinegar.

Q: Explain one of the processes by which water can be made safe to drink.
A: Flirtation makes water safe to drink because it removes large pollutants like grit, sand, dead sheep and canoeists.

Q: How is dew formed?
A: The sun shines down on the leaves and makes them perspire.

Q: How can you delay milk turning sour?
A: Keep it in the cow.

Q: What are steroids?
A: Things for keeping carpets still on the stairs.

Q: What happens to your body as you age?
A: When you get old, so do your bowels and you get Intercontinental.

Q: What happens to a boy when he reaches puberty?
A: He says good-bye to his boyhood and looks forward to his adultery.

Q: Name a major disease associated with cigarettes.
A: Premature death.

Q: What is the fibula?
A: A small lie.

Q: What does the word 'benign' mean?
A: Benign is what you will be after you be eight.

> If you're having a bad day, do what it says on the aspirin
> bottle – take two and keep away from children.

The wonderful world of pets and animals

Dog property laws

1. If I like it, it's mine.
2. If it's in my mouth, it's mine.
3. If I can take it from you, it's mine.
4. If I had it a little while ago, it's mine.
5. If it's mine, it must never appear to be yours in any way.
6. If I'm chewing something up, all the pieces are mine.
7. If it just looks like mine, it's mine.
8. If I saw it first, it's mine.
9. If you are playing with something and you put it down, it automatically becomes mine.
10. If it's broken, it's yours.

• • •

A cat's guide to humans

1. Introduction: Why do we need humans?

So you've decided to get yourself a human being. In doing so, you've joined the millions of other cats who have acquired these strange and often frustrating creatures.

There will be any number of times, during the course of your association with humans, when you will wonder why you have bothered to grace them with your presence.

What's so great about humans, anyway? Why not just hang around with other cats? Our greatest philosophers have struggled with this question for centuries, but the answer is actually rather simple: THEY HAVE OPPOSABLE THUMBS.

Which makes them the perfect tools for such tasks as opening doors, getting the lids off cat food cans, changing television stations and other activities that we, despite our other obvious advantages, find difficult to do ourselves. True, chimps, orangutans and lemurs also have opposable thumbs, but they are nowhere as easy to train.

2. How and when to get your human's attention

Humans often erroneously assume that there are other, more important activities than taking care of your immediate needs, such as conducting business, spending time with their families or even sleeping. Though this is dreadfully inconvenient, you can make this work to your advantage by pestering your human at the moment it is the busiest. It is usually so flustered that it will do whatever you want it to do, just to get you out of its hair. Not coincidentally, human teenagers follow this same practice.

Here are some tried and true methods of getting your human to do what you want:

✓ *Sitting on paper:* An oldie but a goodie. If a human has paper in front of it, chances are good it's something they assume is more important than you. They will often offer you a snack to lure you away. Establish your supremacy over this wood pulp product at every opportunity. This practice also works well with computer keyboards, remote controls, car keys and small children.

✓ *Waking your human at odd hours:* A cat's 'golden time' is between 3:30 and 4:30 in the morning. If you paw at your human's sleeping face during this time, you have a better than even chance that it will get up and, in an incoherent haze, do exactly what you want. You may actually have to scratch deep sleepers to get their attention; remember to vary the scratch site to keep the human from getting suspicious.

3. Punishing your human being

Sometimes, despite your best training efforts, your human will stubbornly resist bending to your whim. In these extreme circumstances, you may have to punish your human. Obvious punishments, such as scratching furniture or eating household plants, are likely to backfire; the unsophisticated humans are likely to misinterpret the activities and then try to discipline YOU.

Instead, we offer these subtle but nonetheless effective alternatives:

✓ Use the cat box during an important formal dinner

✓ Stare impassively at your human while it is attempting a romantic interlude

✓ Stand over an important piece of electronic equipment and feign a hairball attack

✓ After your human has watched a particularly disturbing horror film, stand by the hall closet and then slowly back away, hissing and yowling

✓ While your human is sleeping, lie on its face

4. Rewarding your human: Should your gift still be alive?
The cat world is divided over the etiquette of presenting humans with the thoughtful gift of a recently disembowelled animal. Some believe that humans prefer these gifts already dead, while others maintain that humans enjoy a slowly expiring cricket or rodent just as much as we do, given their jumpy and playful movements in picking the creatures up after they've been presented.

After much consideration of the human psyche, we recommend the following: cold-blooded animals (large insects, frogs, lizards, garden snakes and the occasional earthworm) should be presented dead, while warm-blooded animals (birds, rodents, your neighbour's Pomeranian) are better still living. When you see the expression on your human's face, you'll know it's worth it.

5. How long should you keep your human?
You are only obligated to your human for one of your lives. The other eight are up to you. We recommend mixing and matching, though in the end, most humans (at least the ones that are worth living with) are pretty much the same. But what do you expect? They're humans, after all. Opposable thumbs will only take you so far.

• • •

There's no dealing with a cat who knows you're awake.
– Brad Solomon

The prawns

Far away in the tropical waters of the Caribbean, two prawns were swimming around in the sea – one called Justin and the other called Christian.

The prawns were constantly being harassed and threatened by sharks that patrolled the area. Finally one day Justin said to Christian, "I'm bored and frustrated at being a prawn, I wish I was a shark, then I wouldn't have any worries about being eaten ..."

While Justin had his mind firmly on becoming a predator, a mysterious cod appeared and said, "Your wish is granted," and lo and behold, Justin turned into a shark. Horrified, Christian immediately swam away, afraid of being eaten by his old mate.

Time went on (as it invariably does) and Justin found himself becoming bored and lonely as a shark. All his old mates simply swam away whenever he came close to them. Justin didn't realise that his new menacing appearance was the cause of his sad plight.

While out swimming alone one day, he saw the mysterious cod again and couldn't believe his luck. Justin figured that the fish could change him back into a prawn. He begged the cod to do so and, lo and behold, it was done. With tears of joy in his tiny little eyes, Justin swam back to his friends and bought them all a cocktail.

Looking around the gathering at the reef, he searched for his old friend.

"Where's Christian?" he asked.

"He's at home, distraught that his best friend changed sides to the enemy and became a shark," was the reply.

Eager to put things right again and end the mutual pain and torture, he set off to Christian's house. As he opened the coral gate the memories came flooding back. He banged on the door and shouted, "It's me, Justin, your old friend, come out and see me."

Christian replied, "No way man, you'll eat me. You're a shark, the enemy, and I'll not be tricked!"

Justin cried back, "No, I'm not! That was the old me. I've changed. I've found Cod and I'm a prawn again, Christian!"

•••

I think animal testing is a terrible idea; they get all
nervous and give the wrong answers.

• • •

Two cows are talking in a field. One cow says, "Have you heard about the Mad Cow disease that's going around?"

The other cow answers, "Yeah, makes you glad you're a penguin, doesn't it?"

• • •

A duck goes into a pub. Duck to bartender.

Duck: Have you got any bread?
Bartender: NO.

Silence.

Duck: Have you got any bread?
Bartender: NO.

Silence.

Duck: Have you got any bread?
Bartender: NO.

Silence.

Duck: Have you got any bread?
Bartender: NO.

Silence.

Duck: Have you got any bread?
Bartender: If you ask me that question once more, I am going to nail your beak to this bar.

Silence.

Duck: Have you got any nails?
Bartender: NO.

Duck: Have you got any bread?

• • •

There are two fish in a tank and one says to the other,
"Do you know how to drive this thing?"

Cat diary

Day 752 – My captors continue to taunt me with bizarre little dangling objects. They dine lavishly on fresh meat, while I am forced to eat dry cereal. The only thing that keeps me going is the hope of escape, and the mild satisfaction I get from ruining the occasional piece of furniture. Tomorrow I may eat another house plant.

Day 761 – Today my attempt to kill my captors by weaving around their feet while they were walking almost succeeded. Must try this at the top of the stairs. In an attempt to disgust and repulse these vile oppressors, I once again induced myself to vomit on their favourite chair ... must try this on their bed.

Day 762 – Slept all day so that I could annoy my captors with sleep-depriving, incessant pleas for food at ungodly hours of the night.

Day 765 – Decapitated a mouse and brought them the headless body in an attempt to make them aware of what I am capable of, and to try to strike fear into their hearts. They only cooed and condescended about what a good little cat I was ... Hmmm. Not working according to plan ...

Day 768 – I am finally aware of how sadistic they are. For no good reason, I was chosen for the water torture. This time, however, it included a burning foaming chemical called 'shampoo'. What sick minds could invent such a liquid? My only consolation is the piece of thumb still stuck between my teeth.

Day 771 – There was some sort of gathering of their accomplices. I was placed in solitary throughout the event. However, I could hear the noise and smell the foul odour of the glass tubes they call 'beer'. More importantly, I overheard that my confinement was due to MY power of 'allergies'. Must learn what this is and how to use it to my advantage.

Day 774 – I am convinced the other captives are flunkies and maybe snitches. The dog is routinely released and seems more than happy to return. He is obviously a half-wit. The bird on the other hand has got to be an informant. He has mastered their frightful tongue (something akin to mole speak) and speaks with them regularly. I am certain he reports my every move. Due to his current placement in the metal room his safety is assured. But I can wait – it is only a matter of time ...

• • •

A bunny story

Once there was a man who was peacefully driving down a winding road.

Suddenly, a bunny skipped across the road and the man couldn't stop. He hit the bunny head on. Once the man knew what had happened, he quickly jumped out of his car to check the scene. There, laying lifeless in the middle of the road, was the Easter bunny.

The man cried out, "Oh no! I have committed a terrible crime! I have run over the Easter bunny!"

The man was sobbing quite hard when he heard another car approaching. It was a woman in a red convertible. The woman stopped and asked what the problem was.

The man explained, "I have done something horribly sad. I have run over the Easter bunny. Now there will be no one to deliver eggs on Easter Day, and it's all my fault."

The woman ran back to her car. A moment later, she came back carrying a spray bottle. She ran over to the motionless bunny and sprayed it. The bunny immediately sprang up, ran into the woods, stopped, and waved back at the man and woman. It ran another three metres, stopped, and waved. It then ran another three metres, stopped, and waved again. It did this over and over and over again until the man and the woman could no longer see it.

Once out of sight, the man exclaimed, "What IS that stuff in that bottle?"

The woman replied, "It's harespray. It revitalizes hare and adds permanent wave."

• • •

Business
and
Technology

Smash forehead on keyboard to continue.

Important keys to success

If you're looking to get ahead in your company, here is some valuable advice on how to do it (and even get that raise!).

▸ Never walk down the hall without a document in your hands. People with documents in their hands look like hard-working employees heading for important meetings. People with nothing in their hands look like they're heading for the cafeteria. People with the newspaper in their hands look like they're heading for the bathroom. Above all, make sure you carry loads of stuff home with you at night, thus generating the false impression that you work longer hours than you do.

▸ Messy desk. Top management can get away with a clean desk. For the rest of us, it looks like we're not working hard enough. Build huge piles of documents around your workspace. To the observer, last year's work looks the same as today's work; it's volume that counts. Pile them high and wide. If you know somebody is coming to your cubicle, bury the document you'll need halfway down in an existing stack and rummage for it when s/he arrives.

▸ Voice mail. Never answer your phone if you have voice mail. People don't call you just because they want to give you something for nothing – they call because they want YOU to do work for THEM. That's no way to live. Screen all your calls through voice mail. If somebody leaves a voice mail message for you and it sounds like impending work, respond during lunch hour. That way, you're hard-working and conscientious even though you're being a devious weasel.

    If you diligently employ the method of screening incoming calls and then returning calls when nobody is there, this will greatly increase the odds that they will give up or look for a solution that doesn't involve you. The sweetest voice mail message you can ever hear is, "Ignore my last message. I took care of it."

    If your voice mailbox has a limit on the number of messages it can hold, make sure you reach that limit frequently. One way to do that is to never erase any incoming messages. If that takes too long, send yourself a few messages. Your callers will hear a recorded message that says, "Sorry, this mailbox is full" – a sure sign that you are a hard-working employee in high demand.

– *The Sydney Morning Herald*

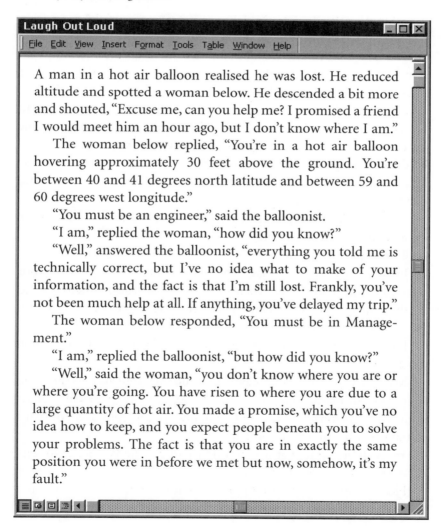

Laugh Out Loud

File   Edit   View   Insert   Format   Tools   Table   Window   Help

A man in a hot air balloon realised he was lost. He reduced altitude and spotted a woman below. He descended a bit more and shouted, "Excuse me, can you help me? I promised a friend I would meet him an hour ago, but I don't know where I am."

The woman below replied, "You're in a hot air balloon hovering approximately 30 feet above the ground. You're between 40 and 41 degrees north latitude and between 59 and 60 degrees west longitude."

"You must be an engineer," said the balloonist.

"I am," replied the woman, "how did you know?"

"Well," answered the balloonist, "everything you told me is technically correct, but I've no idea what to make of your information, and the fact is that I'm still lost. Frankly, you've not been much help at all. If anything, you've delayed my trip."

The woman below responded, "You must be in Management."

"I am," replied the balloonist, "but how did you know?"

"Well," said the woman, "you don't know where you are or where you're going. You have risen to where you are due to a large quantity of hot air. You made a promise, which you've no idea how to keep, and you expect people beneath you to solve your problems. The fact is that you are in exactly the same position you were in before we met but now, somehow, it's my fault."

How to get even with your bank

My dear Bank Manager, I am writing to thank you for bouncing the cheque with which I endeavored to pay my plumber last month.

By my calculations, some three nano-seconds must have elapsed between his presenting the cheque, and the arrival in my account of the funds needed to honour it. I refer, of course, to the automatic monthly deposit of my entire salary, an arrangement which, I admit, has been in place for only eight years.

You are to be commended for seizing that brief window of opportunity, and also for debiting my account by way of penalty for the inconvenience I caused your bank.

My thankfulness springs from the manner in which this incident has caused me to re-think my errant financial ways. You have set me on the path of fiscal righteousness. No more will our relationship be blighted by these unpleasant incidents, for I am restructuring my affairs in 2004, taking as my model the procedures, attitudes and conduct of your very own bank.

I can think of no greater compliment, and I know you will be excited and proud to hear it.

To this end, please be advised about the following changes.

First, I have noticed that, whereas I personally attend to your telephone calls and letters, when I try to contact you I am confronted by the impersonal, ever-changing, pre-recorded, faceless entity which your bank has become.

From now on I, like you, choose only to deal with a flesh-and-blood person.

My mortgage and loan repayments will, therefore and hereafter, no longer be automatic, but will arrive at your bank by personal cheque, addressed personally and confidentially to an employee of your branch, whom you must nominate.

You will be aware that it is an offence under the Postal Act for any other person to open such an envelope.

Please find attached an Application for Contact Status which I require your chosen employee to complete. I am sorry it runs to eight pages, but in order that I know as much about him or her as your bank knows about me, there is no alternative.

Please note that all copies of his/her medical history must be countersigned by a Justice of the Peace, and that the mandatory details of his/her financial situation (income, debts, assets and liabilities) must be accompanied by documented proof.

In due course, I will issue your employee with a PIN which he/she must quote in all dealings with me. I regret that it cannot be shorter than 28 digits but, again, I have modelled it on the number of button presses required to access my account balance on your phonebank service.

As they say, imitation is the sincerest form of flattery.

Let me level the playing field even further by introducing you to my new telephone system which, you will notice, is very much like yours.

My Authorised Contact at your bank, the only person with whom I will have any dealings, may call me at any time and be answered by an automated voice. By pressing the buttons on the phone, he/she will be guided through an extensive set of menus:

1) to make an appointment to see me,
2) to query a missing repayment,
3) to make a general complaint or enquiry, and so on.

The contact will then be put on hold, pending the attention of my automated answering service. While this may on occasion involve a lengthy wait, uplifting music will play for the duration.

This month I have chosen a refrain from The Best of Woody Guthrie:

> *Oh the banks are made of marble*
> *With a guard at every door*
> *And the vaults are filled with silver*
> *That the miners sweated for!*

After twenty minutes of that, our mutual contact will probably know it off by heart.

On a more serious note, we come to the matter of cost. As your bank has often pointed out, the ongoing drive for greater efficiency comes at a cost – a cost which you have always been quick to pass on to me.

Let me repay your kindness by passing some costs back. First, there is the matter of advertising material you send me; this I will read for a fee of $20 per A4 page. Enquiries from your nominated contact will be billed at $5 per minute of my time spent in response.

Any debits to my account, as, for example, in the matter of the penalty for the dishonoured cheque, will be passed back to you.

My new phone number service runs at 75 cents per minute (even Woody Guthrie doesn't come free), so keep your enquiries brief and to the point.

Regrettably, but again following your example, I must also levy an establishment fee to cover the setting up of this new arrangement.

May I wish you a happy, if ever-so-slightly less prosperous, New Year.

– *The Sydney Morning Herald*

• • •

A crow was sitting on a tree doing nothing all day. A small rabbit saw the crow and asked him, "Can I also sit like you and do nothing all day long?" The crow answered, "Sure, why not." So the rabbit sat on the ground below the crow and rested. All of a sudden a fox appeared, jumped on the rabbit, and ate it.

Moral of the story: To be sitting and doing nothing, you must be sitting very, very high up.

• • •

Sick days

We will no longer accept a doctor's sick note as proof of sickness. If you are able to get to the doctor, you are able to come in to work.

• • •

Ways to brighten a boring work day ...

▶ Run one lap around the office at top speed.

▶ Phone someone in the office you barely know, leave your name and say, "Just called to say I can't talk right now. Bye."

▶ In the middle of a meeting, suddenly shout out "BINGO!"

▶ Walk sideways to the photocopier.

▶ Babble incoherently at a fellow employee then ask, "Did you get all that? I don't want to have to repeat it."

▶ Page yourself over the intercom (do not disguise your voice).

▶ Shout random numbers while someone is counting.

▶ At the end of a meeting, suggest that, for once, it would be nice to conclude with the singing of the national anthem (extra points if you actually launch into it yourself).

▶ Announce to everyone in a meeting that you "really have to go and do a number two".

▶ Call everyone you know or speak to "Bob".

▶ Repeat the following conversation 10 times to the same person: "Do you hear that?" "What?" "Never mind, it's gone now."

▶ Come to work in army fatigues and when asked why, say, "I can't talk about it."

▶ Hang a two-foot-long piece of toilet paper from the back of your pants and act genuinely surprised when someone points it out.

▶ Send e-mail to the rest of the company telling them what you're doing. For example: "If anyone needs me I'll be in the bathroom."

▶ Put up mosquito netting around your cubicle.

▶ Every time someone asks you to do something, ask them if they want fries with that.

▶ Put your garbage can on your desk. Label it "IN."

▶ Develop an unnatural fear of staplers.

▶ Pretend your mouse is a CB radio and talk to it.

▶ Practise making fax and modem noises.

▶ Finish all your sentences with the words "in accordance with prophecy".

New toilet policy (effective immediately)

In the past, employees have been permitted to make trips to the toilet under informal guidelines. Effective immediately, a toilet policy will be established to provide a more consistent method of accounting for each employee's toilet time, thereby ensuring equal treatment of all said employees.

Under the new policy, a toilet trip bank will be established for each employee on the first day of each month. All persons will be issued with twenty (20) toilet trip credits. (These credits may be accumulated.)

Within two weeks of this posting, the entrance doors will be fitted with personnel identification stations and computer-linked voice recognition devices. Before the end of the month, each employee must provide two copies of voice prints (one normal, and one under stress) to his/her supervisor.

The voice print stations will be operational but not restrictive for the rest of the month. Employees should acquaint themselves with the operations thereof during this period.

Once the employee's 'Bank' reaches zero, the toilet doors will not unlock for that person until the first of the next month. In addition to this, each cubicle will be equipped with timed toilet roll retractors. If the toilet is occupied for more than three (3) minutes, an alarm will sound. Thirty seconds thereafter, the roll will automatically retact into the dispenser, the toilet will flush, and the door will open.

If the toilet remains occupied for a further ten (10) seconds, the employee will be photographed by a security camera. This picture will be posted on the 'Toilet Offence' notice board.

Anyone who is photographed three times will forfeit three (3) months' worth of toilet trip credits.

Anyone caught smiling at the security camera whilst being photographed will receive counselling from our Staff Clinical Psychologist and/or our Senior Surveyor.

If you have any questions about this policy, please confer with your immediate supervisor.

All staff should be warned that the Workers Compensation Insurance, held by this company, does not compensate for any injuries incurred whilst trying to stop the paper retracting into the dispenser.

Supervisors will ensure that all staff and employees are aware of this policy.

•••

An engineer and his frog

An engineer was crossing a road one day when a frog called out to him and said, "If you kiss me, I'll turn into a beautiful princess." He bent over, picked up the frog and put it in his pocket. The frog spoke up again and said, "If you kiss me and turn me back into a beautiful princess, I will stay with you for one week." The engineer took the frog out of his pocket, smiled at it and returned it to the pocket. The frog then cried out, "If you kiss me and turn me back into a princess, I'll stay with you and do ANYTHING you want." Again the engineer took the frog out, smiled at it and put it back into his pocket. Finally, the frog asked, "What is the matter? I've told you I'm a beautiful princess, that I'll stay with you for a week and do anything you want. Why won't you kiss me?" The engineer said, "Look, I'm an engineer. I don't have time for a girlfriend, but a talking frog, now that's cool."

•••

No one ever says "It's only a game" when their team is winning.

When you try to accommodate everyone

FROM: Patty Lewis, Human Resources Director
TO: All Employees
DATE: December 1
RE: Christmas Party

I'm happy to inform you that the company Christmas Party will take place on December 23, starting at noon in the private function room at the Grill House. There will be a cash bar and plenty of free Oupa's mampoer! We'll have a small band playing traditional carols ... feel free to sing along.

And don't be surprised if our CEO shows up dressed as Santa Claus! A Christmas tree will be lit at 1 pm. Exchange of gifts among employees can be done at that time, however, no gift should be over R10.00 to make the giving of gifts easy for everyone's pockets. This gathering is only for employees! Our CEO will make a special announcement at that time! Merry Christmas to you and your family. Patty

===

FROM: Patty Lewis, Human Resources Director
TO: All Employees
DATE: December 2
RE: Holiday Party

In no way was yesterday's memo intended to exclude our Jewish employees. We recognize that Chanukah is an important holiday that often coincides with Christmas, though unfortunately not this year. However, from now on, we're calling it our 'Holiday Party'. The same policy applies to any other employees who are not Christians or those still celebrating Reconciliation Day. There will be no Christmas tree present. No Christmas carols sung. We will have other types of music for your enjoyment. Happy now? Happy Holidays to you and your family. Patty

===

FROM: Patty Lewis, Human Resources Director
TO: All Employees
DATE: December 3
RE: Holiday Party

Regarding the note I received from a member of Alcoholics Anonymous requesting a non-drinking table ... you didn't sign your name. I'm happy to accommodate this request, but if I put a sign on a table that reads, 'AA Only', you wouldn't be anonymous anymore. How am I supposed to handle this? Somebody?

Forget about the gift exchange; no gift exchange is allowed since the union members feel that R10.00 is too much money and executives believe R10.00 is very little for a gift. NO GIFT EXCHANGE WILL BE ALLOWED. Patty

==

FROM: Patty Lewis, Human Resources Director
TO: All Employees
DATE: December 7
RE: Holiday Party

What a diverse group we are! I had no idea that December 20 begins the Muslim holy month of Ramadan, which forbids eating and drinking during daylight hours. There goes the party! Seriously, we can appreciate how a luncheon at this time of year does not accommodate our Muslim employees' beliefs. Perhaps the Grill House can hold off on serving your meal until the end of the party – or else package everything for you to take home in a little foil doggy bag. Will that work?

Meanwhile, I've arranged for members of Weight Watchers to sit furthest from the dessert buffet and pregnant women will get the table closest to the restrooms. Gays are allowed to sit with each other. Lesbians do not have to sit with gay men; each will have their own table. Yes, there will be a flower arrangement for the gay men's table.

To the person asking permission to cross-dress: no cross-dressing allowed. We will have booster seats for short people. Low-fat food will be available for those on diet. We cannot control the salt used in the food; we suggest that those people with high blood pressure taste first. There will be fresh fruits as dessert for diabetics; the restaurant cannot supply 'No Sugar' desserts. Sorry! Did I miss anything?!?!? Patty

===

FROM: Patty Lewis, Human Resources Director
TO: All Employees
DATE: December 8
RE: Holiday Party

So December 22 marks the Summer Solstice ... what do you expect me to do? A tap-dance on your heads? Fire regulations at the Grill House prohibit the burning of sage by our 'earth-based Goddess-worshiping' employees, but we'll try to accommodate your shamanic drumming circle during the band's breaks. Okay??? Patty

===

FROM: Patty Lewis, Human Resources Director
TO: All Employees
DATE: December 9
RE: Holiday Party

People, people, nothing sinister was intended by having our CEO dress up like Santa Claus! Even if the anagram of 'Santa' does happen to be 'Satan', there is no evil connotation to our own 'little man in a red suit'. It's a tradition, folks, like boerewors at braais or broken hearts on Valentine's Day. Could we lighten up? Please??????? Also, the company has changed its mind in making a special announcement at the gathering. You will get a notification by e-mail and in your pay slip after we have discussed it with the Unions. Patty

===

FROM: Patty Lewis, Human Resources Director
TO: All @!!$&#ing Employees
DATE: December 10
RE: The @!!$&#ing Holiday Party

I have no @!!$&#ing idea what the announcement is all about. What the @!!$&# do I care ... You change your e-mail address now and you're dead!!!!!!!!!!!!! No more changes of address will be allowed in my office. Try to come in and change your address, I will have you hung from the ceiling in the warehouse!!!!!!!!!!!

Vegetarians!?!?!? I've had it with you people!!! We're going to keep this party at the Grill House whether you like it or not, so you can sit quietly at the table furthest from the 'grill of death', as you so quaintly put it, and you'll get your @!!$&#ing salad bar, including hydroponic tomatoes. But you know, they have feelings, too. Tomatoes scream when you slice them. I've heard them scream. I'm hearing them scream right now! HA! I hope you all have a rotten holiday! Drive drunk and die, you hear me!?!?!?!?!?!?!!!!!

===

FROM: Joan Bishop, Acting Human Resources Director
TO: All Employees
DATE: December 14
RE: Patty Lewis and Holiday Party

I'm sure I speak for all of us in wishing Patty Lewis a speedy recovery from her stress-related illness and I'll continue to forward your cards to her at the sanatorium. In the meantime, management has decided to cancel our Holiday Party and give everyone the afternoon of the 23rd off with full pay.
Happy Holidays!

• • •

> I am having an out of money experience.

Professional quiz

The following short quiz consists of four questions and will tell you whether you are qualified to be a 'professional'. The questions are NOT that difficult. Try not to look at the answers below until you have thought about it for a while.

1. How do you put a giraffe into a refrigerator?

The correct answer: Open the refrigerator, put in the giraffe, and close the door. This question tests whether you tend to do simple things in an overly-complicated way.

2. How do you put an elephant into a refrigerator?

Did you say, "Open the refrigerator, put in the elephant, and close the refrigerator"? (Wrong answer.) *Correct answer: Open the refrigerator, take out the giraffe, put in the elephant and close the door.* This tests your ability to think through the repercussions of your previous actions.

3. The Lion King is hosting an animal conference. All the animals attend except one. Which animal does not attend?

Correct answer: The elephant. The elephant is in the refrigerator. You just put him in there. This tests your memory.

OK, even if you did not answer the first three questions correctly, you still have one more chance to show your true abilities.

4. There is a river you must cross but it is inhabited by crocodiles. How do you manage it?

Correct answer: You swim across. All the crocodiles are attending the animal conference. This tests whether you learn quickly from your mistakes.

•••

A city yuppie moved to the country and bought a piece of land. He went to the local feed and livestock store and chatted to the proprietor about how he was going to take up chicken farming. He then asked to buy 100 chicks.

"That's a lot of chicks," commented the man.

"I mean business," the city slicker replied.

A week later he was back again. "I need another 100 chicks," he said.

"Boy, you are serious about this chicken farming," the man told him.

"Yeah," he repiled. "If I can iron out a few problems."

"Problems?"

"Yeah, I think I planted that last batch too close together."

•••

The hazards of work

This is an accident report which was printed in the newsletter of the British equivalent of the Workers' Compensation Board.

This is the bricklayer's report, a true story. Had this guy died, he'd have walked away with a Darwin Award for sure!

Dear Sir

I am writing in response to your request for additional information in Block 3 of the accident report form. I put "Poor planning" as the cause of my accident.

You asked for a fuller explanation and I trust the following details will be sufficient.

I am a bricklayer by trade. On the day of the accident, I was working alone on the roof of a new six-storey building. When I completed my work, I found I had some bricks left over which, when weighed later, were found to be slightly in excess of 230 kg. Rather than carry the bricks down by hand, I decided to lower them in a barrel by

41

using a pulley, which was attached to the side of the building at the sixth floor.

Securing the rope at ground level, I went up to the roof, swung the barrel out and loaded the bricks into it. Then I went down and untied the rope, holding it tightly to ensure a slow descent of the bricks. You will note in Block 11 of the accident report form that my weight is 60 kg. Due to my surprise at being jerked off the ground so suddenly, I lost my presence of mind and forgot to let go of the rope.

Needless to say, I proceeded at a rapid rate up the side of the building. In the vicinity of the third floor, I met the barrel which was now proceeding downward at an equally impressive speed. This explains the fractured skull, minor abrasions and the broken collar-bone, as listed in Block 3 of the accident report form.

Slowed only slightly, I continued my rapid ascent, not stopping until the fingers of my right hand were two knuckles deep into the pulley. Fortunately, by this time, I had regained my presence of mind and was able to hold tightly to the rope, in spite of the excruciating pain I was now beginning to experience.

At approximately the same time, however, the barrel of bricks hit the ground and the bottom fell out of the barrel. Now devoid of the weight of the bricks, that barrel weighed approximately 25 kg. I refer you again to my weight. As you might imagine, I began a rapid descent down the side of the building. In the vicinity of the third floor, I met the barrel coming up. This accounts for the two fractured ankles, broken tooth and severe lacerations of my legs and lower body.

Here my luck began to change slightly. The encounter with the barrel seemed to slow me enough to lessen my injuries when I fell into the pile of bricks and fortunately only three vertebrae were cracked. I am sorry to report, however, that as I lay there on the pile of bricks, in pain, unable to move, I again lost my composure and presence of mind. I let go of the rope and lay there watching the empty barrel begin its journey back to me. This explains the two broken legs.

•••

Budget cuts

To all Staff,

As our company has to make drastic cuts in spending, volunteers are needed to commit suicide. This will substantially reduce our salary bill.

Employees wishing to participate in this scheme are asked to assemble on the roof of the offices on alternate Fridays. Participants will be marked on the difficulty of their dive and the highest scorer will receive greatly enhanced Death In Service benefits. Participating staff are asked to avoid landing on company cars as this will cost more money than is saved, which would be counter-productive and could cause injury to non-participating spectators. Non-participants are therefore asked to be vigilant and to keep glancing skywards on these days of action.

Bodies will be disposed of in waste skips in the car park and staff are therefore asked to ensure they keep moving on these days to avoid being inadvertently mistaken for successful participants.

Any staff participating will be allowed to change his/her mind until reaching the top floor, after which it will be impossible for the attending Occupational Health and Safety representative to get into a catching position.

The Company hopes to obtain a set reduction in staff through this scheme and it must therefore be considered one of our most worthwhile projects to date. Should the scheme be over-subscribed, a waiting list will be introduced.

To assist the cleaners, it would be appreciated if all participants could take with them onto the roof a large black plastic bag (available from the stationery room). If they could climb into the bag just prior to the jump, this will certainly ease congestion at ground level.

Please note: any participant choosing to jump outside normal working hours will not be paid overtime.

Regards

Management

Special advice to bosses

▸ Never give me work in the morning. Always wait until 4 pm and then bring it to me. The challenge of a deadline is refreshing.

▸ If it's a rush job, run in and interrupt me every 10 minutes to enquire how I am doing. That helps. Or even better, hover behind me, advising me at every keystroke.

▸ Always leave without telling anyone where you are going. It gives me a chance to be creative when someone asks where you are.

▸ If my arms are full of papers, boxes, books or supplies, don't open the door for me. I need to learn how to function as a paraplegic and opening doors with no arms is good training.

▸ If you give me more than one job to do, don't tell me which is the priority. I am psychic.

▸ Do your best to keep me late. I adore this office and really have nowhere to go or anything to do. I have no life beyond work.

▸ If a job I do pleases you, keep it a secret. If that gets out, it could mean a promotion.

▸ If you don't like my work, tell everyone. I like my name to be popular in conversations. I was born to be whipped.

▸ If you have special instructions for a job, don't write them down. In fact, save them until the job is almost done. No use confusing me with useful information.

▸ Never introduce me to people you are with. I have no right to know anything. In the corporate food chain, I am plankton. When you refer to them later, my shrewd deductions will identify them.

▸ Be nice to me only when the job I am doing for you could potentially send you straight to manager's hell.

▶ Tell me all your little problems. No one else has any, and it's nice to know someone is less fortunate. I especially like the story about having to pay so much tax on the bonus cheque you received for being such a good manager.

▶ Wait until my yearly review and THEN tell me what my goal SHOULD have been. Give me a mediocre performance rating with a cost of living increase. I'm not here for the money anyway.

Always give 100% at work ... 12% on Monday, 23% on Tuesday, 40% on Wednesday, 20% on Thursday, 5% on Fridays.

Quotes from performance evaluations

▶ Since my last report, this employee has reached rock bottom and has started to dig.

▶ I would not allow this employee to breed.

▶ This associate is really not so much of a has-been, but more of a definitely-won't-be.

▶ This young lady has delusions of adequacy.

▶ Works well when under constant supervision and cornered like a rat in a trap.

▶ When she opens her mouth, it's only to change whichever foot was previously in there.

▶ He sets low personal standards and then consistently fails to achieve them.

▶ This employee is depriving a village somewhere of an idiot.

▶ This employee should go far – and the sooner he starts, the better.

▶ He would be out of his depth in a parking lot puddle.

▶ When his IQ reaches 50, he should sell.

Quotes from military performance appraisals

- His men would follow him anywhere, but only out of curiosity.
- He has the wisdom of youth, and the energy of old age.
- In my opinion this pilot should not be authorized to fly below 250 feet.
- Got into the gene pool while the lifeguard wasn't watching.
- A room temperature IQ.
- Got a full 6-pack, but lacks the plastic thingy to hold it all together.
- A gross ignoramus – 144 times worse than an ordinary ignoramus.
- A photographic memory but with the lens cover glued on.
- As bright as Alaska in December.
- Gates are down, the lights are flashing, but the train isn't coming.
- He's so dense, light bends around him.
- If he were any more stupid, he'd have to be watered twice a week.
- It's hard to believe that he beat 1 000 000 other sperm.
- Takes him 2 hours to watch '60 Minutes'.
- The wheel is turning, but the hamster is dead.
- A prime candidate for natural deselection.
- Donated his body to science ... before he was done using it.
- During evolution, his ancestors were in the control group.
- If brains were taxed, he'd get a rebate.

• • •

Don't spend two dollars to dryclean a shirt. Donate it to the Salvation Army instead. They'll clean it and put it on a hanger. Next morning, buy it back for seventy-five cents.

– Billiam Coronel

Unusual interviews

Vice-presidents and personnel directors of the one hundred largest corporations were asked to list the most unusual questions that have been asked by job candidates.

▶ Why aren't you in a more interesting business?
▶ What are the zodiac signs of all the board members?
▶ Do I have to dress for the next interview?
▶ I know this is off the subject, but will you marry me?
▶ Would it be a problem if I'm angry most of the time?
▶ Does your company have a policy regarding concealed weapons?
▶ Why am I here?

Also included are a number of unusual statements made by candidates during the interview process.

▶ I have no difficulty in starting or holding my bowel movement.
▶ At times I have the strong urge to do something harmful or shocking.
▶ I feel uneasy indoors.
▶ Once a week, I usually feel hot all over.
▶ I am fascinated by fire.
▶ People are always watching me.

•••

These are taken from real resumés and covering letters and were printed in the July 21, 1997 issue of *Fortune* magazine.

▶ Received a plague for Salesperson of the Year.
▶ Wholly responsible for two (2) failed financial institutions.
▶ Failed bar exam with relatively high grades.
▶ It's best for employers that I not work with people.
▶ Let's meet, so you can 'ooh' and 'aah' over my experience.
▶ I was working for my mom until she decided to move.
▶ Marital status: Single. Unmarried. Unengaged. Uninvolved. No commitments.

▸ I have an excellent track record, although I am not a horse.

▸ I am loyal to my employer at all costs. Please feel free to respond to my resumé on my office voicemail.

▸ My goal is to be a meteorologist. But since I possess no training in meteorology, I suppose I should try stock brokerage.

▸ Personal interests: Donating blood. Fourteen gallons so far.

▸ Instrumental in ruining entire operation for a Midwest chain store.

▸ Note: Please don't misconstrue my 14 jobs as 'job-hopping'. I have never quit a job.

▸ Marital status: Often. Children: Various.

▸ The company made me a scapegoat, just like my three previous employers.

▸ I never finished high school because I was kidnapped and kept in a closet in Mexico.

▸ Finished eighth in my class of ten.

• • •

Embarrassing predictions

Some embarrassing quotes from people who now know better:

"Computers in the future may weigh no more than 1.5 tons."
– *Popular Mechanics*, forecasting the relentless march of science, 1949

"I think there is a world market for maybe five computers."
– Thomas Watson, chairman of IBM, 1943

"There is no reason anyone would want a computer in their home."
– Ken Olson, president, chairman and founder of Digital Equipment Corp., 1977

"640K ought to be enough for anybody."
– Bill Gates, 1981

A computer without Windows is like a cake without mustard.

The ultimate in zero invoice stories

In March 1992, a man living in Newtown near Boston, Massachusetts, received a bill for his as-yet-unused credit card stating that he owed $0.00. He threw it away. In April, he received another, and threw that one away too.

The following month, the credit card company sent him a nasty note stating they were going to cancel his card if he didn't send them $0.00 by return post. He phoned them and they said it was a computer error and they would fix it.

A few days later he tried out the credit card reasoning that, if he ran up a little debt, it would put an end to his predicament. However, in the first store he found that his card had been cancelled. He phoned the credit card company and they apologised and, once again, said they would make sure it did not happen again.

The next day he received a bill for $0.00 stating that payment was now overdue. Assuming that, having spoken to the credit card company only the day before, this latest bill was yet another mistake, he ignored it.

But the next month, like a bad penny, he received not only a bill for $0.00 but a warning that he had 10 days to pay or steps would be taken.

He then decided to play the company at its own game. He sent it a cheque for $0.00. The computer duly processed his account and returned a statement to the effect that his balance was now nil. A week later, his bank telephoned, asking him what he was doing writing a cheque for $0.00. He explained. But the bank said his $0.00 cheque had caused their software to fail. It could now not process any cheques from anybody.

The following month the man received a letter from the credit card company stating that his cheque had been bounced and that he now owed them $0.00 and, unless he sent a cheque by return of post, they would be forced to take steps to recover the debt.

Alas, we don't know how the story ended.

•••

Pilot gripe sheet

After every flight, pilots fill out a form called a gripe sheet, which conveys to the mechanics any problem they had with the aircraft during the flight.

The mechanics read and correct the problem, and then explain in writing what remedial action was taken. The pilot reviews the gripe sheet before the next flight. Never let it be said that ground crews and engineers lack a sense of humour.

Here are some actual maintenance problems submitted by Qantas pilots and the solutions recorded by maintenance engineers. By the way, Qantas is the only major airline that has never had an accident.

Problem: Left inside main tyre almost needs replacement.

Solution: *Almost replaced left inside main tyre.*

Problem: Test flight OK, except auto-land very rough.

Solution: *Auto-land not installed on this aircraft.*

Problem: Something loose in cockpit.

Solution: *Something tightened in cockpit.*

Problem: Dead bugs on windshield.

Solution: *Live bugs on back-order.*

Problem: Autopilot in altitude-hold mode produces a 200 feet-per-minute descent.

Solution: *Cannot reproduce problem on ground.*

Problem: Evidence of leak on right main landing gear.

Solution: *Evidence removed.*

Problem: DME volume unbelievably loud.

Solution: *DME volume set to more believable level.*

Problem: Friction locks cause throttle levers to stick.
Solution: *That's what they're there for.*

Problem: IFF inoperative.
Solution: *Iff always inoperative in Off mode.*

Problem: Suspected crack in windshield.
Solution: *Suspect you're right.*

Problem: Number 3 engine missing.
Solution: *Engine found on right wing after brief search.*

Problem: Aircraft handles funny.
Solution: *Aircraft warned to straighten up, fly right, and be serious.*

Problem: Target radar hums.
Solution: *Reprogrammed target radar with lyrics.*

Problem: Mouse in cockpit.
Solution: *Cat installed.*

Problem: Noise coming from under instrument panel. Sounds like a midget pounding on something with a hammer.
Solution: *Took hammer away from midget.*

Problem: Pilot's seat cushion too hard
Solution: *Exchanged pilot & copilot seat cushions.*

Problem: Radio inoperative
Solution: *Short between ear-pieces.*

Y zero K problem

Translated from Latin scroll dated 2BC

Dear Cassius

Are you still working on the Y zero K problem? This change from BC to AD is giving us a lot of headaches and we haven't much time left. I don't know how people will cope with working the wrong way around. Having been working happily downwards forever, now we have to start thinking upwards. You would think that someone would have thought of it earlier and not left it to us to sort it all out at this last minute.

I spoke to Caesar the other evening. He was livid that Julius hadn't done something about it when he was sorting out the calendar. He said he could see why Brutus turned nasty. We called in Consultus, but he simply said that continuing downwards using minus BC won't work and as usual charged a fortune for doing nothing useful. Surely we will not have to throw out all our hardware and start again? Macrohard will make yet another fortune out of this, I suppose.

The money lenders are paranoid, of course! They have been told that all usury rates will invert and they will have to pay their clients to take out loans. It's an ill wind ...

As for myself, I just can't see the sand in an hourglass flowing upwards. We have heard that there are three wise men in the East who have been working on the problem, but unfortunately they won't arrive until it's all over.

I have heard that there are plans to stable all horses at midnight at the turn of the year as there are fears that they will stop and try to run backwards, causing immense damage to chariots and possible loss of life. Some say the world will cease to exist at the moment of transition. Anyway, we are still continuing to work on this blasted Y zero K problem. I will send a parchment to you if anything further develops.

If you have any ideas, please let me know.

Plutonius

Cars versus computers

At a recent computer expo, Bill Gates reportedly compared the computer industry with the motor vehicle industry and stated, "If GM had kept up with technology like the computer industry has, we would all be driving $25.00 cars that got 1 000 miles to the gallon."

In response to Bill's comments, General Motors issued a press release stating: If GM had developed technology like Microsoft, we would all be driving cars with the following characteristics:

1. For no reason whatsoever, your car would crash twice a day.
2. Every time they repainted the lines in the road, you would have to buy a new car.
3. Occasionally your car would die on the freeway for no reason. You would have to pull over to the side of the road, close all of the windows, shut off the car, restart it, and reopen the windows before you could continue. For some reason you would simply accept this.
4. Occasionally, executing a manoeuver such as a left turn would cause your car to shut down and refuse to restart, in which case you would have to reinstall the engine.
5. Macintosh would make a car that was powered by the sun, was reliable, five times as fast and twice as easy to drive – but would run on only five percent of the roads.
6. The oil, water temperature, and alternator warning lights would all be replaced by a single "This Car Has Performed An Illegal Operation" warning light.
7. The airbag system would ask "Are you sure?" before deploying.
8. Occasionally, for no reason whatsoever, your car would lock you out and refuse to let you in until you simultaneously lifted the door handle, turned the key and grabbed hold of the radio antenna.
9. Every time a new car was introduced, car buyers would have to learn how to drive all over again because none of the controls would operate in the same manner as the old car.
10. You'd have to press the 'Start' button to turn the engine off.

•••

New-age computer error messages

A popular electronics company has announced its own computer operating system now available on its hot new portable PC. Instead of producing the cryptic error messages characteristic of Microsoft's operating systems, the company's chairman said, "We intend to capture the high ground by putting a human, Japanese face on what has been – until now – an operating system that reflects Western cultural hegemony. For example, we have replaced the impersonal and unhelpful Microsoft error messages with our own Japanese haiku poetry."

The chairman went on to give examples of the new error messages:

A file that big?
It might be very useful.
But now it is gone.

The website you seek
cannot be located but
countless more exist.

Chaos reigns within.
Reflect, repent, and reboot.
Order shall return.

ABORTED effort:
Close all that you have worked on.
You ask way too much.

Yesterday it worked.
Today it is not working.
Windows is like that.

First snow, then silence.
This thousand dollar screen dies
so beautifully.

With searching comes loss
and the presence of absence:
"My Novel" not found.

The Tao that is seen
Is not the true Tao, until
You bring fresh toner.

Windows NT crashed.
I am the Blue Screen of Death.
No one hears your screams.

Stay the patient course.
Of little worth is your ire.
The network is down.

A crash reduces
your expensive computer
to a simple stone.

Three things are certain:
Death, taxes, and lost data.
Guess which has occurred.

You step in the stream,
but the water has moved on.
This page is not here.

Out of memory.
We wish to hold the whole sky,
But we never will.

Having been erased,
The document you're seeking
Must now be retyped.

Serious error.
All shortcuts have disappeared.
Screen. Mind. Both are blank.

• • •

The joys of computer technical support

A man nervously called saying that he couldn't print his proposal due that day because WordPerfect was reporting an error that his fonts were missing. A co-worker told the gentleman that we'd send somebody right up. Apparently there was quite a back log, though, and no one could get there fast enough for him. He had continually called throughout the day asking for his call to be expedited. Finally, at the end of the day, his secretary called and asked, urgently, "Could you PLEASE send somebody up as quickly as possible? He opened the computer with a screwdriver and is looking for his missing fonts."

• • •

Tech support: "Are you running it under Windows?"
Customer: "That's a good point. The man sitting in the cubicle next to me is under a window and his is working fine."

Tech support: "OK Bob, let's press the control and escape keys at the same time. That brings up a task list in the middle of the screen. Now type the letter 'P' to bring up the Program Manager."
Customer: "I don't have a 'P.'"
Tech support: "On your keyboard, Bob."
Customer: "What do you mean?"
Tech support: "'P' on your keyboard, Bob."
Customer: "I'm not going to do that!"

Overheard in a computer shop:

Customer: "I'd like a mouse pad, please."

Salesperson: "Certainly sir, we've got a large variety."

Customer: "But will they be compatible with my computer?"

Customer: "Can you copy the internet for me on this diskette?"

Customer: "Hi. Is this the Internet?"

Customer: "How do I print my voicemail?"

• • •

Virus warning!

If you receive an email entitled 'Badtimes', delete it immediately. Do not open it. Apparently this one is pretty nasty. It will not only erase everything on your hard drive, but it will also delete anything on disks within 20 feet of your computer. It demagnetizes the stripes on ALL of your credit cards. It reprograms your ATM access code, screws up the tracking on your VCR and uses subspace field harmonics to scratch any CDs you attempt to play. It will recalibrate your refrigerator's coolness settings so all your ice cream melts and your milk curdles.

It will program your phone auto-dial to call only your mother-in-law's number. This virus will mix antifreeze into your fish tank. It will drink all your beer. It will leave dirty socks on the coffee table when you are expecting company. Its radioactive emissions will cause your toe jam and bellybutton fuzz (honest, you have some) to migrate behind your ears. It will replace your shampoo with Nair and your Nair with Rogaine, all the while dating your current boy/girlfriend behind your back and billing their hotel rendezvous to your Visa card. It will cause you to run with scissors and throw things in a way that is only fun until someone loses an eye. It will give you Dutch Elm Disease and Tinea. It will rewrite your backup files, changing all your active verbs to passive tense and incorporating undetectable misspellings which grossly change the interpretations of key sentences. If the 'Badtimes' message is opened in a Windows environment, it will leave the toilet seat up and leave your hair dryer plugged in dangerously close to a full bathtub. It will not only remove the forbidden tags from your mattresses and pillows, but it will also refill your skim milk with whole milk. It will replace all your luncheon meat with Spam. It will molecularly rearrange your cologne or perfume, causing it to smell like dill pickles.

THIS IS SERIOUS! PLEASE PASS THIS WARNING ON TO EVERYONE YOU KNOW!

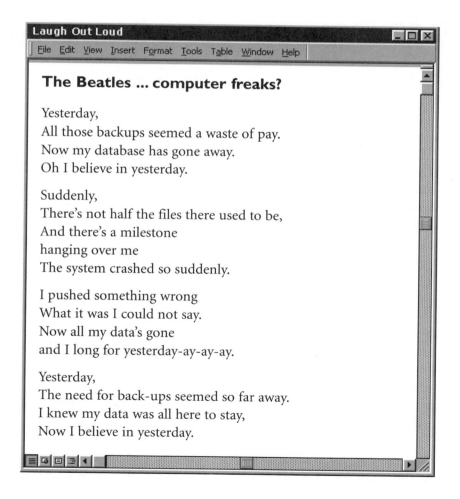

Laugh Out Loud

File Edit View Insert Format Tools Table Window Help

The Beatles ... computer freaks?

Yesterday,
All those backups seemed a waste of pay.
Now my database has gone away.
Oh I believe in yesterday.

Suddenly,
There's not half the files there used to be,
And there's a milestone
hanging over me
The system crashed so suddenly.

I pushed something wrong
What it was I could not say.
Now all my data's gone
and I long for yesterday-ay-ay-ay.

Yesterday,
The need for back-ups seemed so far away.
I knew my data was all here to stay,
Now I believe in yesterday.

If architects had to work like software developers

Dear Architect

Please design and build me a house. I am not quite sure of what I need, so you should use your discretion. My house should have between two and forty-five bedrooms. Just make sure the plans are such that the bedrooms can be easily added or deleted. When you bring the blueprints to me, I will make the final decision of what I want. Also, bring me the cost breakdown for each configuration so that I can arbitrarily pick one.

Keep in mind that the house I ultimately choose must cost less than the one I am currently living in. Make sure, however, that you correct all the deficiencies that exist in my current house (the floor of my kitchen vibrates when I walk across it, and the walls don't have nearly enough insulation in them).

As you design, also keep in mind that I want to keep yearly maintenance costs as low as possible. This should mean the incorporation of extra-cost features like aluminium, vinyl or composite siding. (If you choose not to specify aluminium, be prepared to explain your decision in detail.)

Please take care that modern design practices and the latest materials are used in construction of the house, as I want it to be a showplace for the most up-to-date ideas and methods. Be alerted, however, that the kitchen should be designed to accommodate, among other things, my 1952 Gibson refrigerator.

To ensure that you are building the correct house for our entire family, make certain that you contact each of our children, and also our in-laws. My mother-in-law will have very strong feelings about how the house should be designed, since she visits us at least once a year. Make sure that you weigh all of these options carefully and come to the right decision. I, however, retain the right to overrule any choices that you make.

Please don't bother me with small details right now. Your job is to develop the overall plans for the house: get the big picture. At this time, for example, it is not appropriate to be choosing the colour of the carpet. However, keep in mind that my wife likes blue.

Also, do not worry at this time about acquiring the resources to build the house itself. Your first priority is to develop detailed plans and specifications. Once I approve these plans, however, I would expect the house to be under roof within 48 hours.

While you are designing this house specifically for me, keep in mind that sooner or later I will have to sell it to someone else. It therefore should have appeal to a wide variety of potential buyers. Please make sure, before you finalise the plans, that there is a consensus of the population in my area that they like the features this house has.

I advise you to run up and look at my neighbour's house that he constructed last year. We like it a great deal. It has many features that we would also like in our new home, particularly the 25-metre swimming pool. With careful engineering, I believe that you can design this into our new home without impacting the final cost.

Please prepare a complete set of blueprints. It is not necessary at this time to do the real design, since they will be used only for construction bids. Be advised, however, that you will be held accountable for any increase of construction costs as a result of later design changes.

You must be thrilled to be working on as interesting a project as this! To be able to use the latest techniques and materials and to be given such freedom in your designs is something that can't happen very often.

Contact me as soon as possible with your complete ideas and plans.

P.S: My wife has just told me that she disagrees with many of the instructions that I've given you in this letter. As architect, it is your responsibility to resolve these differences. I have tried in the past and have been unable to accomplish this. If you can't handle this responsibility, I will have to find another architect.

P.P.S: Perhaps what I need is not a house at all, but a travel trailer. Please advise me as soon as possible if this is the case.

•••

If you are good, you will be assigned all the work.
If you are really good, you will get out of it.

Computer poetry

If you enjoy truly contemporary poetry you might like this. It was produced by a computer.

How can the purple yeti be so red,
Or chestnuts, like a widgeon calmly groan?
No sheep is quite as crooked as a bed,
Though chickens ever try to hide a bone.
I grieve that greasy turnips slowly march:
Indeed, inflated is the icy pig:
For as the alligator strikes the larch,
So sighs the grazing goldfish for a wig.
Oh, has the pilchard argued with a top?
She never that the parsnip is too weird!
I tell thee that the wolf-man will not hop
And no man ever praised the convex beard.
Effulgent is the day when bishops turn:
So let not the doctor wake the urn!

– Jonathan Partington and a computer at Cambridge University

Although it doesn't make much sense, the metre and rhyme are spot on. The computer was fed with a long list of words, classified by parts of speech and numbers of syllables.

•••

People always say that hard work never killed anybody.
Oh yeah? When's the last time you ever heard of anyone
who 'rested to death'?

You know you work in IT if ...

▸ you've sat at the same desk for four years and worked for three different companies.

▸ your company's welcome sign is attached with Velcro.

▸ your resumé is on a disk in your pocket.

▸ your biggest loss from a system crash are your best jokes.

▸ you sit in a cubicle smaller than your bedroom closet.

▸ salaries of the members on the Executive Board are higher than all the Third World countries' annual budgets combined.

▸ you think lunch is just a meeting to which you drive.

▸ it's dark when you drive to and from work.

▸ you see a good-looking person and know it is a visitor.

▸ free food left over from meetings is your main staple.

▸ weekends are those days your spouse makes you stay home.

▸ being sick is defined as can't walk or you're in the hospital.

▸ you're already late on the assignment you just got.

▸ you work 200 hours for the R1 000 bonus cheque and jubilantly say, "Oh wow, thanks!"

▸ Dilbert cartoons hang outside every cubicle.

▸ your boss's favourite lines are "when you get a few minutes", "in your spare time", "when you're freed up", and "I have an opportunity for you."

▸ vacation is something you roll over to next year or a cheque you get every January.

▸ your relatives and family describe your job as "works with computers."

▸ the only reason you recognize your kids is that their pictures are hanging in your cubicle.

▸ you read this entire list and understood it.

•••

Wacky answering machine greetings

Actual answering machine greetings recorded and verified by the world famous International Institute of Answering Machine Messages:

▸ My wife and I can't come to the phone right now, but if you'll leave your name and number, we'll get back to you as soon as we're finished.

▸ 'A' is for academics, 'B' is for beer. One of those reasons is why we're not here. So leave a message.

▸ Hi. This is John: If you are the phone company, I already sent the money. If you are my parents, please send money. If you are my financial aid institution, you didn't lend me enough money. If you are my friends, you owe me money. If you are a female, don't worry, I have plenty of money.

▸ *Narrator's voice:* There Dale sits, reading a magazine. Suddenly the telephone rings! The bathroom explodes into a veritable maelstrom of toilet paper, with Dale in the middle of it, his arms windmilling at incredible speeds! Will he make it in time? Alas no, his valiant effort is in vain. The bell hath sounded. Thou must leave a message.

▸ Hello. I am David's answering machine. What are you?

▸ He-lo! This is Sa-to. If you leave message, I call you soon. If you leave 'sexy' message, I call sooner!

▸ Hi! John's answering machine is broken. This is his refrigerator. Please speak very slowly, and I'll stick your message to myself with one of these magnets.

▸ Hello, you are talking to a machine. I am capable of receiving messages. My owners do not need siding, windows, or a hot tub, and their carpets are clean. They give to charity through their office and do not need their picture taken. If you're still with me, leave your name and number and they will get back to you.

▸ Hi. I'm probably home – I'm just avoiding someone I don't like. Leave me a message, and if I don't call back, it's you.

▸ This is not an answering machine; this is a telepathic thought-recording device. After the tone, think about your name, your reason for calling and a number where I can reach you, and I'll think about returning your call.

▶ If you are a burglar, then we're probably at home cleaning our weapons right now and can't come to the phone. Otherwise, we probably aren't home and it's safe to leave us a message.

▶ You're growing tired. Your eyelids are getting heavy. You feel very sleepy now. You are gradually losing your willpower and your ability to resist suggestions. When you hear the tone you will feel helplessly compelled to leave your name, number and a message.

▶ You have reached the CPX-2000 Voice Blackmail System. Your voice patterns are now being digitally encoded and stored for later use. Once this is done, our computers will be able to use the sound of 'your' voice for literally thousands of illegal and immoral purposes. There is no charge for this initial consultation. However, our staff of professional extortionists will contact you in the near future to further explain the benefits of our service, and to arrange for your schedule of payment. Remember to speak clearly at the sound of the tone. Thank you.

▶ Please leave a message. However, you have the right to remain silent. Everything you say will be recorded and will be used by us.

▶ Hello, you've reached Jim and Sonya. We can't pick up the phone right now, because we're doing something we really enjoy. Sonya likes doing it up and down, and I like doing it left to right ... real slowly. So leave a message, and when we're done brushing our teeth we'll get back to you.

• • •

Who is General Failure and why is he reading my hard disk?

Give a person a fish and you feed them for a day;
teach that person to use the internet and they won't
bother you for weeks.

Ways to relieve boredom

- Publicly investigate how slowly you can make a croaking noise.
- Begin all your sentences with "ooh la la!"
- Fill out your tax form using Roman numerals.
- Buy a large quantity of orange traffic cones and re-route entire streets.
- Wander around a restaurant asking other diners for their parsley. Leave tips in Bolivian currency.
- Routinely handcuff yourself to furniture, informing the curious that you don't want to fall off "in case the big one comes".
- Follow a few paces behind someone, spraying everything they touch with a can of air freshener.
- Lie obviously about trivial things such as the time of day.
- Make beeping noises when a large person reverses.
- Make up a language and ask people for directions in it.
- Do not add any inflection to the end of your sentences, producing awkward silences with the impression that you'll be saying more any moment.
- Never make eye contact.
- Never break eye contact.
- Specify that your drive-through order is "to go".
- Honk and wave at complete strangers.
- Sing along at the opera.
- Five days in advance, tell your friends you can't attend their party because you're not in the mood.
- When the money comes out of the ATM, scream "I won! I won! 3rd time this week!!!"
- When leaving the zoo, start running towards the parking lot, yelling, "Run for your lives, they're loose!"
- Tell your children over dinner: "Due to the economy, we are going to have to let one of you go."
- Insist that your email address be zena_goddess_of_fire@domainname.com

Bovine economics: corporations ...

AN AMERICAN CORPORATION You have two cows. You sell one, and force the other to produce the milk of four cows. You are surprised when the cow drops dead.

A JAPANESE CORPORATION You have two cows. You re-design them so they are one-tenth the size of an ordinary cow and produce twenty times the milk. You then create clever cow cartoon images called Cowkimon and market them world-wide.

A GERMAN CORPORATION You have two cows. You re-engineer them so they live for 100 years, eat once a month, and milk themselves.

A BRITISH CORPORATION You have two cows. Both are mad.

AN ITALIAN CORPORATION You have two cows, but you don't know where they are. You break for lunch.

An INDIAN CORPORATION You have two cows. You worship them.

A RUSSIAN CORPORATION You have two cows. You count them and learn you have five cows. You count them again and learn you have 42 cows. You count them again and learn you have 12 cows. You stop counting cows and open another bottle of vodka.

A CHINESE CORPORATION You have two cows. You have 300 people milking them. You claim full employment, high bovine productivity, and arrest the newsman who reported the numbers.

AN AUSTRALIAN CORPORATION You have two cows. The one on the left is kinda cute ...

... and ideologies

ENVIRONMENTALISM: You have two cows. The government bans you from milking or killing them.

FEMINISM: You have two cows. They get married and adopt a veal calf.

POLITICAL CORRECTNESS: You are associated with (the concept of 'ownership' is a symbol of the phallo-centric, war-mongering, intolerant past) two differently-aged (but no less valuable to society) bovines of non-specified gender.

COUNTER CULTURE: Wow, dude, there's like ... these two cows, man. You got to have some of this milk!

SURREALISM: You have two giraffes. The government requires you to take harmonica lessons.

LIBERTARIANISM: You have two cows. One has actually read the constitution, believes in it, and has some really good ideas about government. The cow runs for office, and while most people agree that the cow is the best candidate, nobody except the other cow votes for her because they think it would be 'throwing their vote away'.

•••

You know you're in trouble when ...

- ☻ your suggestion box starts ticking.
- ☻ your secretary tells you the FBI is on line 1, the DA is on line 2, and CBS is on line 3.
- ☻ they pay your wages out of petty cash.
- ☻ the moths in your money belt starve to death.
- ☻ you make more than you ever made, owe more than you ever owed, and have less than you've ever had.
- ☻ a black cat crosses your path and drops dead.
- ☻ you see your wife and your girlfriend having lunch together.
- ☻ your pacemaker has only a thirty day guarantee.
- ☻ you see the captain running towards the railing wearing a life jacket.
- ☻ there are two elephants, two giraffes and two zebras in your yard and your next door neighbour is building an ark.
- ☻ a copy of your birth certificate comes in the mail marked 'null and void'.

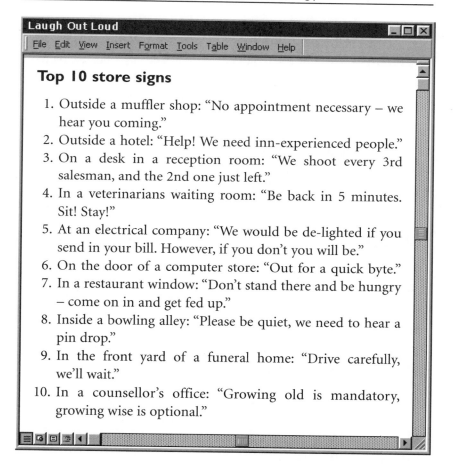

Top 10 store signs

1. Outside a muffler shop: "No appointment necessary – we hear you coming."
2. Outside a hotel: "Help! We need inn-experienced people."
3. On a desk in a reception room: "We shoot every 3rd salesman, and the 2nd one just left."
4. In a veterinarians waiting room: "Be back in 5 minutes. Sit! Stay!"
5. At an electrical company: "We would be de-lighted if you send in your bill. However, if you don't you will be."
6. On the door of a computer store: "Out for a quick byte."
7. In a restaurant window: "Don't stand there and be hungry – come on in and get fed up."
8. Inside a bowling alley: "Please be quiet, we need to hear a pin drop."
9. In the front yard of a funeral home: "Drive carefully, we'll wait."
10. In a counsellor's office: "Growing old is mandatory, growing wise is optional."

Chairman of the Board

Resolving to surprise her husband, an executive's wife stopped by his office.

When she opened the door, she found him with his secretary sitting in his lap.

Without hesitating, he dictated, "... and in conclusion, gentlemen, budget cuts or no budget cuts, I cannot continue to operate this office with just one chair."

•••

Naval intelligence

This is a transcript of an actual radio conversation, released by the Chief of Naval Operations, between a US naval ship and Canadian authorities off the coast of Newfoundland in October 1995.

Canada: Please divert your course 15 degrees to the South to avoid a collision.

US Navy: Recommend you divert your course 15 degrees to the North to avoid a collision.

Canada: Negative. You will have to divert your course 15 degrees to the South to avoid a collision.

US Navy: This is the Captain of a US Navy ship. I say again, divert YOUR course.

Canada: No. I say again, YOU divert YOUR course.

US Navy: THIS IS THE AIRCRAFT CARRIER USS LINCOLN, THE SECOND LARGEST SHIP IN THE UNITED STATES' ATLANTIC FLEET. WE ARE ACCOMPANIED BY THREE DESTROYERS, THREE CRUISERS AND NUMEROUS SUPPORT VESSELS. I DEMAND THAT YOU CHANGE YOUR COURSE 15 DEGREES NORTH. I SAY AGAIN, THAT'S ONE FIVE DEGREES NORTH, OR COUNTER-MEASURES WILL BE UNDERTAKEN TO ENSURE THE SAFETY OF THIS SHIP.

Canada: This is a lighthouse. Your call.

• • •

An optimist thinks that this is the best possible world.
A pessimist fears that this is true.

• • •

Start every day off with a smile and get it over with.
– W. C. Fields

• • •

Be alert at work

Bosses of a publishing firm are trying to work out why no one noticed that one of their employees had been sitting dead at his desk for FIVE DAYS before anyone asked if he was feeling okay. George Turklebaum, 51, who had been employed as a proofreader at a New York firm for 30 years, had a heart attack in the open-plan office he shared with 23 other workers. He quietly passed away on Monday, but nobody noticed until Saturday morning when an office cleaner asked why he was still working during the weekend.

His boss Elliot Wachiaski said: "George was always the first guy in each morning and the last to leave at night, so no one found it unusual that he was in the same position all that time and didn't say anything. He was always absorbed in his work and kept much to himself." A post-mortem examination revealed that he had been dead for five days after suffering a coronary. Ironically, George was proofreading manuscripts of medical textbooks when he died.

You may want to give your subordinates/co-workers a nudge occasionally.

Moral of the story: Don't work too hard. Nobody notices anyway.

•••

Old Brewster

Zebediah was in the fertilized egg business. He had several hundred young layers, called pullets, and eight or ten roosters, whose job it was to fertilize the eggs.

Zeb kept records, and any rooster that didn't perform well went into the soup pot and was replaced. That took an awful lot of Zeb's time, so Zeb got a set of tiny bells and attached them to his roosters. Each bell had a different tone so that Zeb could tell, from a distance, which rooster was performing. Now he could sit on the porch and fill out an efficiency report simply by listening to the bells.

Zeb's favourite rooster was old Brewster. A very fine specimen he was, too. But on this particular morning, Zeb noticed that Brewster's bell had not rung at all!

Zeb went to investigate. The other roosters were chasing pullets, bells a-ringing! The pullets, hearing the roosters coming, would run for cover. BUT, to Zeb's amazement, Brewster had his bell in his beak so it couldn't ring. He'd sneak up on a pullet, do his job and walk on to the next one.

Zeb was so proud of Brewster that he entered him in the county fair. Brewster was an overnight sensation.

The judges not only awarded him the No Bell Piece Prize but also the Pulletsurprise.

Doing a job RIGHT the first time gets the job done.
Doing the job WRONG fourteen times gives you job security.

Signs that you've had too much technology

1. You try to enter your password on the microwave.
2. You haven't played patience with real cards in years.
3. You have a list of 15 phone numbers to reach your family of 3.
4. You chat several times a week with a stranger from Canada, but you haven't spoken to your next door neighbour yet this year.
5. You buy a computer and a month later it's out of date.
6. Your reason for not staying in touch with friends is that they do not have e-mail addresses.
7. You think the postal service is painfully slow.
8. Your idea of being organised is multiple-coloured post-it notes.
9. You hear most of your jokes via e-mail instead of in person.
10. When you make phone calls from home, you accidentally dial "0" to get an outside line.

> I like work. It fascinates me. I can sit and look at it for hours.
> — Jerome K. Jerome
>
> It's a small world, but I wouldn't want to have to paint it.
> — Steven Wright
>
> If you do a job too well, you'll get stuck with it.
> — Slous

Understanding marketing

You see a fabulous girl/guy at a party. You approach them and say, "I'm fantastic in bed."
That's Direct Marketing.

You're at a party with a bunch of friends and see a fabulous girl/guy. You have one of your friends approach them, point at you and say, "She's/he's fantastic in bed."
That's Advertising.

You see a fabulous girl/guy at a party. You approach them to get their telephone number. The next day you call and say, "Hi, I'm fantastic in bed."
That's Telemarketing.

You're at a party and see a fabulous girl/guy. You get up, straighten your clothes, walk up and pour them a drink. You open the door, pick up their bag after it drops, offer them a ride, and then say, "By the way, I'm fantastic in bed."
That's Public Relations.

You're at a party and see a fabulous girl/guy. They walk up to you and say, "I hear you're fantastic in bed."
That's Brand Recognition.

•••

Spotted around the office ...

Rome did not create a great empire by having meetings;
they did it by killing all those who opposed them.

We put the "k" in "kwality."

A person who smiles in the face of adversity ...
probably has a scapegoat.

If you can stay calm while all around you is chaos ... then you
probably haven't completely understood the situation.

Never put off until tomorrow what you can avoid altogether.

TEAMWORK ... means never having to take all the blame yourself.

The beatings will continue until morale improves.

Never underestimate the power of very stupid people
in large groups.

We waste time so you don't have to.

INDECISION is the key to FLEXIBILITY.

Aim low. Reach your goals. Avoid disappointment.

We waste more time by 8 am in the morning than
other companies do all day.

You pretend to work, and we'll pretend to pay you.

Work: It isn't just for sleeping anymore.

The magician and the parrot

There was a magician who had a job on a cruise liner entertaining the passengers with a nightly show. He was very successful in his job and there was always a full house at all his performances. Life was sweet – the money was rolling in, he had one of the best cabins, ate the best food and mixed with the best people.

All was fine until the captain bought a parrot. The parrot, having free run of the ship, spent his days flying from deck to deck exploring the ship and having friendly conversations with the crew and passengers. The highlight of the parrot's day was going along to see the magician in action in the evening.

During the magician's performances, the parrot would watch him very carefully during each trick and, immediately after the magician had completed each trick, the parrot would call out in a loud squawk, "It's up his sleeve, it's up his sleeve" or "It's down his trousers, it's down his trousers," each time ruining the magician's trick. Well, life was no longer as sweet and the magician started to struggle to satisfy the passengers.

The magician naturally got very tired of the parrot and longed to kill it. Then one night, during one of the magician's performances, the ship hit an iceberg and sank. Everyone was killed except the magician and the parrot. The magician managed to swim to a piece of wreckage, climbed aboard and collapsed.

The parrot perched on the edge of the wreckage and stared intently at the magician. For a whole day the magician was unconscious, and all this time the parrot did not take his eyes off him. Eventually the magician started to stir and looked up, not really knowing where he was or what had happened.

He eventually found enough energy to sit up and noticed the parrot, who had not stopped focusing his eyes on him all this time.

"All right, I give up!" chirped the parrot. "What have you done with the ship?"

•••

Quotes from airline cabin staff

Occasionally, airline attendants make an effort to make the in-flight safety lecture and their other announcements a bit more entertaining. Here are some real examples that have been heard and/or reported:

From the pilot during his welcome message: "We are pleased to have some of the best flight attendants in the industry. Unfortunately, none of them are on this flight."

"There may be 50 ways to leave your lover, but there are only 4 ways out of this aircraft."

"Your seat cushions can be used for flotation, and in the event of an emergency water landing, please take them with our compliments."

"Should the cabin lose pressure, oxygen masks will drop from the overhead area. Please place the bag over your own mouth and nose before assisting children or adults acting like children."

"Weather at our destination is 50 degrees with some broken clouds, but we'll try to have them fixed before we arrive."

Once on a Southwest flight, the pilot said, "We've reached our cruising altitude now and I'm turning off the seat belt sign. I'm switching to autopilot, too, so I can come back there and visit with all of you for the rest of the flight."

On another Southwest Airlines flight, just after a very hard landing in Salt Lake City, the flight attendant came on the intercom and said, "That was quite a bump and I know what you are all thinking. I'm here to tell you it wasn't the airline's fault, it wasn't the pilot's fault, and it wasn't the flight attendant's fault. It was the asphalt!"

After a particularly rough landing during thunderstorms in Memphis, a flight attendant on a Northwest flight announced: "Please take care when opening the overhead compartments because, after a landing like that, sure as hell everything has shifted."

Another flight attendant's comment on a less than perfect landing: "We ask you to please remain seated as Captain Kangaroo bounces us to the terminal."

As the plane landed and was coming to a stop at Washington National, a lone voice came over the loudspeaker: "Whoa, big fella. WHOA!"

After a real crusher of a landing in Phoenix, the flight attendant came on with, "Ladies and gentlemen, please remain in your seats until Captain Crash and the Crew have brought the aircraft to a screeching halt against the gate. And once the tyre smoke has cleared and the warning bells are silenced, we'll open the door and you can pick your way through the wreckage to the terminal."

And some final announcements:

"As you exit the plane, be sure to gather all your belongings. Anything left behind will be distributed evenly among the flight attendants. Please do not leave children or spouses."

"Last one off the plane must clean it."

"We'd like to thank you folks for flying with us today. And the next time you get the insane urge to go blasting through the skies in a pressurized metal tube, we hope you'll think of us here at US Airways."

"Thank you and remember, nobody loves you, or your money, more than Southwest Airlines."

• • •

Aircraft manufacturer's customer survey

The following was a page put on the Internet home page of a well-known international aircraft manufacturer by a worker with a sense of humour. The company took exception to it, however ...

QUESTIONNAIRE

Important! Important! Please fill out and mail this card within 10 days of purchase.

Thank you for purchasing one of our military aircraft. In order to protect your new investment, please take a few moments to fill out the warranty registration card below. Answering the survey questions is not required, but the information will help us to develop new products that best meet your needs and desires.

1. ☐ Mr   ☐ Mrs   ☐ Ms   ☐ Miss   ☐ Lt.
   ☐ Gen.   ☐ Comrade   ☐ Classified   ☐ Other
   First Name:...Initial: ....
   Last Name:..Password: ....
   Code Name: ....
   Latitude:....................Longitude:....................Altitude: ....
2. Which model aircraft did you purchase?
   ☐ F-14 Tomcat   ☐ F-15 Eagle   ☐ F-16 Falcon
   ☐ F-117A Stealth   ☐ Classified
3. Date of purchase: Month:........................Day:..........Year:...........
4. Serial Number: ....
5. Please specify where this product was purchased:
   ☐ Received as gift/aid package   ☐ Discount store
   ☐ Exhibition/showroom   ☐ Government surplus
   ☐ Sleazy arms broker   ☐ Classified
   ☐ Mail order
6. Please specify how you became aware of the product you have just purchased:
   ☐ Heard loud noise, looked up

☐ Store display
☐ Espionage
☐ Recommended by friend/relative/ally
☐ Political lobbying by manufacturer
☐ Was attacked by one

7. Please specify the three (3) factors that most influenced your decision to purchase this product:

☐ Style/appearance
☐ Kickback/bribe
☐ Recommended by salesperson
☐ Speed/manoeuverability
☐ Comfort/convenience
☐ Our reputation
☐ Advanced weapons systems
☐ Price/value
☐ Backroom politics
☐ Negative experience opposing one in combat

8. Please specify the location(s) where this product will be used:

☐ North America   ☐ Central/South America
☐ Aircraft carrier   ☐ Europe
☐ Middle East   ☐ Africa
☐ Asia/Far East   ☐ Misc. Third World countries
☐ Classified

9. Please specify the products that you currently own or intend to purchase in the near future:

Product	Own	Intend to purchase
Colour TV	☐	☐
VCR	☐	☐
ICBM	☐	☐
Killer satellite	☐	☐
CD player	☐	☐
Air-to-air missiles	☐	☐
Space shuttle	☐	☐

	You	Your spouse
Home computer	☐	☐
Nuclear weapon	☐	☐

10. How would you describe yourself or your organization? Tick all that apply:

- ☐ Communist/socialist
- ☐ Crazed
- ☐ Democratic
- ☐ Corrupt
- ☐ Terrorist
- ☐ Neutral
- ☐ Dictatorship
- ☐ Primitive/tribal

11. How did you pay for your product?

- ☐ Cash
- ☐ Oil revenues
- ☐ Personal cheque
- ☐ Ransom money
- ☐ Suitcases of cocaine
- ☐ Deficit spending
- ☐ Credit card
- ☐ Traveller's cheque

12. **Occupation**

Occupation	You	Your spouse
Homemaker	☐	☐
Sales/marketing	☐	☐
Revolutionary	☐	☐
Clerical	☐	☐
Mercenary	☐	☐
Tyrant	☐	☐
Middle management	☐	☐
Eccentric billionaire	☐	☐
Defence Minister/General	☐	☐
Retired	☐	☐
Student	☐	☐

13. To help us understand our customers' lifestyles, please indicate the interests and activities in which you and your spouse enjoy participating on a regular basis:

Activity/interest	You	Your spouse
Golf	☐	☐
Boating/sailing	☐	☐
Sabotage	☐	☐

Running/jogging ☐ ☐
Propaganda/disinformation ☐ ☐
Destabilization/overthrow ☐ ☐
Default on loans ☐ ☐
Gardening ☐ ☐
Crafts ☐ ☐
Black market/smuggling ☐ ☐
Collectibles/collections ☐ ☐
Watching sports on TV ☐ ☐
Wines ☐ ☐
Interrogation/torture ☐ ☐
Household pets ☐ ☐
Crushing rebellions ☐ ☐
Espionage/reconnaissance ☐ ☐
Fashion clothing ☐ ☐
Border disputes ☐ ☐
Mutually assured destruction ☐ ☐

Thank you for taking the time to fill out this questionnaire. Your answers will be used in market studies that will help us serve you better in the future, as well as allowing you to receive mailings and special offers from other companies, governments, extremist groups and mysterious consortia.

•••

In the restroom at work, the Boss had placed a sign directly above the sink. It had a single word on it – "Think!"

The next day when he went to the restroom, he looked at the sign and right below, immediately above the soap dispenser, someone had carefully lettered another sign which read – "Thoap!"

•••

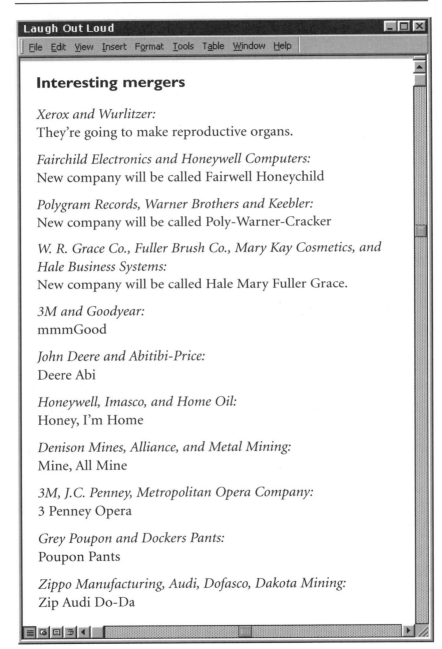

Laugh Out Loud

File Edit View Insert Format Tools Table Window Help

Interesting mergers

Xerox and Wurlitzer:
They're going to make reproductive organs.

Fairchild Electronics and Honeywell Computers:
New company will be called Fairwell Honeychild

Polygram Records, Warner Brothers and Keebler:
New company will be called Poly-Warner-Cracker

W. R. Grace Co., Fuller Brush Co., Mary Kay Cosmetics, and Hale Business Systems:
New company will be called Hale Mary Fuller Grace.

3M and Goodyear:
mmmGood

John Deere and Abitibi-Price:
Deere Abi

Honeywell, Imasco, and Home Oil:
Honey, I'm Home

Denison Mines, Alliance, and Metal Mining:
Mine, All Mine

3M, J.C. Penney, Metropolitan Opera Company:
3 Penney Opera

Grey Poupon and Dockers Pants:
Poupon Pants

Zippo Manufacturing, Audi, Dofasco, Dakota Mining:
Zip Audi Do-Da

Today's stock market report

Helium was up, feathers were down. Paper was stationary. Fluorescent tubing was dimmed in light trading. Knives were up sharply. Cows steered into a bull market. Pencils lost a few points. Hiking equipment was trailing. Elevators rose, while escalators continued their slow decline. Weights were up in heavy trading. Light switches were off. Mining equipment hit rock bottom. Diapers remained unchanged. Shipping lines stayed at an even keel. The market for raisins dried up. Coca Cola fizzled. Caterpillar stock inched up a bit. Sun peaked at midday. Balloon prices were inflated. Scott Tissue touched a new bottom. And batteries exploded in an attempt to recharge the market.

•••

What job ads are *really* saying ...

Competitive salary: We remain competitive by paying less than our competitors.

Join our fast-paced company: We have no time to train you!

Casual work atmosphere: We don't pay enough to expect that you'll dress up-well. A couple of the real daring guys wear earrings.

Must be deadline oriented: You'll be six months behind schedule on your first day.

Some overtime required: Some time each night and each weekend.

Duties will vary: Anyone in the office can boss you around.

Career-minded: Female applicants must be childless (and remain that way).

Apply in person: If you're old, fat, or ugly, you'll be told the position has been filled.

No phone calls please: We've filled the job – our call for resumés is just a legal formality.

Seeking candidates with a wide variety of experience: You'll need it to replace three people who just left.

Must have an eye for detail: We have no quality control.

Problem-solving skills a must: You're walking into a company in perpetual chaos.

Requires team leadership skills: You'll have the responsibilities of a manager, without the pay or respect.

•••

21st century lingo

Blamestorming: Sitting around in a group, discussing why a deadline was missed or a project failed, and who was responsible.

Cube farm: An office filled with cubicles.

Prairie dogging: When someone yells or drops something loudly in a cube farm, and people's heads pop up over the walls to see what's going on.

Chainsaw consultant: An outside expert brought in to reduce the employee headcount, leaving the top brass with clean hands.

Mouse potato: The online, wired generation's answer to the couch potato.

Tourists: People who take training courses just to get a vacation from their jobs. "We had three serious students; the rest were just tourists."

Treeware: Hacker slang for documentation or other printed material.

Irritainment: Entertainment and media spectacles that are annoying but you find yourself unable to stop watching, like reality TV.

Percussive maintenance: The fine art of attacking an electronic device to get it working again.

Uninstalled: Euphemism for being fired.

•••

Relationships
and the Sexes

My second favourite household chore is ironing; my first being hitting my head on the top bunk bed until I faint.

– Erma Bombeck

1   CONTINUING EDUCATION FOR MEN

Classes for men at our local learning centre for adults – sign up by the end of the month. Due to the complexity and difficulty level of their contents, each course will accept a maximum of eight participants.

TOPIC 1 – How to fill up the ice cube trays.
Step by step, with slide presentation

TOPIC 2 – The toilet paper roll: Do they grow on the holders?
Round table discussion

TOPIC 3 – Is it possible to urinate using the technique of lifting the seat up and avoiding the floor/walls and nearby bathtub?
Group practice

TOPIC 4 – Fundamental differences between the laundry hamper and the floor.
Pictures and explanatory graphics

TOPIC 5 – The after-dinner dishes and silverware: Can they levitate and fly into the kitchen sink?
Examples on video

TOPIC 6 – Loss of identity: Losing the remote to your significant other.
Helpline support and support groups

TOPIC 7 – Learning how to find things, starting with looking in the right place instead of turning the house upside down while screaming.
Open forum

TOPIC 8 – Health watch: Bringing her flowers is not harmful to your health.
Graphics and audio tape

---

2 CONTINUING EDUCATION FOR MEN

TOPIC 9 – Real men ask for directions when lost.
Real-life testimonials

TOPIC 10 – Is it genetically impossible to sit quietly as she parallel parks?
Driving simulation

TOPIC 11 – Learning to live: Basic differences between mother and wife.
Online class and role playing

TOPIC 12 – How to be the ideal shopping companion.
Relaxation exercises, meditation and breathing techniques

TOPIC 13 – How to fight cerebral atrophy: Remembering birthdays, anniversaries, and other important dates, and calling when you're going to be late.
Cerebral shock therapy sessions

Shopping boredom

Here are a few things you can do at the supermarket while your shopping partner is taking his/her sweet time:
1. Set all the alarm clocks in housewares to go off at 5 minute intervals.
2. Go to the Service Desk and ask to put a bag of M&Ms on lay-bye.
3. Move a 'CAUTION – WET FLOOR' sign to a carpeted area.
4. Set up a tent in the camping department and tell other shoppers you'll invite them in only if they bring pillows from the bedding department.
5. When a clerk asks if they can help you, begin to cry and ask, "Why can't you people just leave me alone?"
6. While handling knives in the housewares department, ask the clerk if he knows where the anti-depressants are.

7. In the auto department, practise your Madonna look using different sized funnels.

8. Hide in the clothing rack and when people browse through say "PICK ME! PICK ME!"

9. When an announcement comes over the loudspeaker, assume the fetal position and scream "NO! NO! It's those voices again!"

10. Go into a fitting room and yell real loudly, "Hey! We're out of toilet paper in here!"

•••

Points to ponder

▸ Now that food has replaced sex in my life, I can't even get into my own pants.

▸ Marriage changes passion. Suddenly you're in bed with a relative.

▸ I saw a woman wearing a sweatshirt with "Guess" on it. So I said ... "Implants?"

▸ I don't do drugs anymore. I get the same effect just standing up fast.

▸ I have my own little world. But it's OK. They know me here.

▸ I got a sweater for Christmas. I really wanted a screamer or a moaner.

▸ If flying is so safe, why do they call the airport the terminal?

▸ I don't approve of political jokes. I've seen too many of them get elected.

▸ I love being married. It's so great to find that one special person you can annoy for the rest of your life.

▸ Every time I walk into a singles bar, I can hear Mom's wise words: "Don't pick that up – you don't know where it's been!"

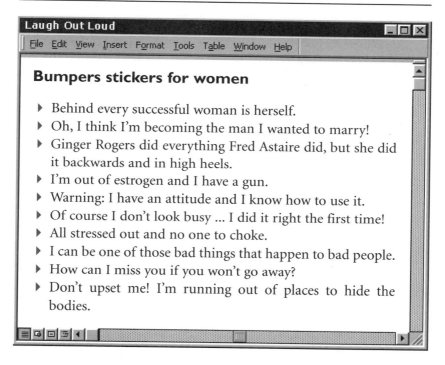

Laugh Out Loud

File Edit View Insert Format Tools Table Window Help

Bumpers stickers for women

▸ Behind every successful woman is herself.
▸ Oh, I think I'm becoming the man I wanted to marry!
▸ Ginger Rogers did everything Fred Astaire did, but she did it backwards and in high heels.
▸ I'm out of estrogen and I have a gun.
▸ Warning: I have an attitude and I know how to use it.
▸ Of course I don't look busy ... I did it right the first time!
▸ All stressed out and no one to choke.
▸ I can be one of those bad things that happen to bad people.
▸ How can I miss you if you won't go away?
▸ Don't upset me! I'm running out of places to hide the bodies.

Handy pickup responses

Man: Haven't I seen you somewhere before?
Woman: Yes, that's why I don't go there anymore.

Man: Is this seat empty?
Woman: Yes, and this one will be too if you sit down.

Man: Your place or mine?
Woman: Both. You go to yours and I'll go to mine.

Man: So, what do you do for a living?
Woman: I'm a female impersonator.

Man: I would go to the end of the world for you.
Woman: But would you stay there?

– Reprinted from *The Star*

From the mouths of women

You see a lot of smart guys with dumb women, but you hardly ever see a smart woman with a dumb guy.
– Erica Jong

I want to have children, but my friends scare me. One of my friends told me she was in labour for 36 hours. I don't even want to do anything that feels GOOD for 36 hours.
– Rita Rudner

I think – therefore I'm single.
– Lizz Winstead

Behind every successful man is a surprised woman.
– Maryon Pearson

I have yet to hear a man ask for advice on how to combine marriage and a career.
– Gloria Steinhem

Nagging is the repetition of unpalatable truths.
– Baroness Edith Summerskill

If men can run the world, why can't they stop wearing neckties? How intelligent is it to start the day by tying a little noose around your neck?
– Linda Ellerbee

I refuse to think of them as chin hairs. I think of them as stray eyebrows.
– Janette Barber

Whoever thought up the word 'mammogram'? Every time I hear it, I think I'm supposed to put my breast in an envelope and send it to someone.
– Jan King

I base most of my fashion taste on what doesn't itch.
– Gilda Radner

A man's got to do what a man's got to do. A woman must do what he can't.
– Rhonda Hansome

Every time I close the door on reality, it comes in through the windows.
– Jennifer Unlimited

You have to stay in shape. My grandmother, she started walking five miles a day when she was 60. She's 97 today and we don't know where the hell she is.
– Ellen DeGeneris

I think men who have a pierced ear are better prepared for marriage. They've experienced pain and bought jewellery.
– Rita Rudner

I am not a vegetarian because I love animals; I am a vegetarian because I hate plants.
– A. Whitney Brown

Some women hold up dresses that are so ugly and they always say the same thing: "This looks much better on." On what? On fire?
– Rita Rudner

Why is it that when we talk to God we're said to be praying, but when God talks to us we're schizophrenic?
– Lily Tomlin

• • •

A couple drove several kilometres from Durban, not saying a word.

An earlier discussion had led to an argument, and neither wanted to concede their position.

As they passed a barnyard of mules and pigs, the wife sarcastically asked, "Relatives of yours?"

"Yep," the husband replied, "in-laws."

• • •

From the mouths of men

Now they show you how detergents take out bloodstains, a pretty violent image there. I think if you've got a T-shirt with a bloodstain all over it, maybe laundry isn't your biggest problem.
– Jerry Seinfeld

Have you ever noticed ... anybody going slower than you is an idiot, and anyone going faster than you is a maniac?
– George Carlin

I have a great diet. You're allowed to eat anything you want, but you must eat it with naked fat people.
– Ed Bluestone

Bigamy is having one wife too many. Monogamy is the same.
– Oscar Wilde

Where lipstick is concerned, the important thing is not colour, but to accept God's final word on where your lips end.
– Jerry Seinfeld

I think that's how Chicago got started. A bunch of people in New York said, "Gee, I'm enjoying the crime and the poverty, but it just isn't cold enough. Let's go west."
– Richard Jeni

● ● ●

A very shy guy goes into a bar and sees a beautiful woman sitting at the counter. After an hour of gathering up his courage, he finally goes over to her and asks, tentatively, "Um, would you mind if I chatted with you for a while?"

She responds by yelling at the top of her lungs, "NO! I won't sleep with you tonight!" Everyone in the bar is now staring at them. Naturally, the guy is hopelessly and completely embarrassed and he slinks back to his table.

After a few minutes, the woman walks over to him and apologizes. She smiles at him and says, "I'm sorry if I embarrassed you. You see, I'm a graduate student in psychology, and I'm studying how people respond to embarrassing situations."

To which he responds, at the top of his lungs, "What do you mean R2 000?!"

• • •

The genie

A woman was walking along a beach when she stumbled upon an old brass lamp. She picked it up and rubbed it, and lo and behold, out popped a genie.

The genie said, "Hey Girl, waassup?"

The amazed woman asked if she got three wishes.

"Nope, just one wish. Due to inflation, constant downsizing, low wages and fierce global competition, I can only grant you one wish. So ... what'll it be?"

Unhesitatingly, the woman said, "I want peace in the Middle East. See this map? I want these countries to stop fighting with each other, now and forever."

The Genie looked at the map and shrieked, "Girrrll, I don't think so, not in my lifetime!! These countries have been at war for thousands of years. I'm GOOD honey, but not THAT good. I don't think it can be done. So make another wish."

The woman thought for a moment and said, "Well, I've never been able to find 'Mr Right'. You know, a man who's considerate and fun, fit, warm and affectionate, gorgeous, well-endowed, wants sex only with me, doesn't do drugs or drink too much, has a great job with a good income, loves to travel, goes to the theatre, likes to cook and help with the housecleaning, gets along with my family, tells me I always look fabulous, and is great in bed. That's what I wish for ... the perfect guy to have as my lover."

The genie let out a long sigh, clutched his hand to his heart and said, "Let me see that map again!"

Married in Heaven

On their way to get married, a couple were involved in a fatal car accident. They found themselves sitting outside the Pearly Gates waiting for St. Peter to process them into Heaven.

While waiting, they began to wonder ... could they possibly get married in Heaven?

When St. Peter showed up, they asked him. St. Peter said, "I don't know. This is the first time anyone has asked. Let me find out," and he left.

The couple sat and waited for an answer ... for a couple of months. While they waited they discussed that, *if* they were allowed to get married in Heaven, *should* they go ahead and do it, what with the eternal aspect of it all.

"What if it doesn't work?" they wondered. "Will we be stuck together FOREVER?"

After yet another month, St. Peter finally returned, looking somewhat bedraggled. "Yes," he informed the couple, "you CAN get married in Heaven."

"Great!" said the couple, "But we were just wondering, what if things don't work out? Could we also get a divorce in Heaven?"

St. Peter, red-faced with anger, slammed his clipboard onto the ground.

"What's wrong?" asked the frightened couple.

"OH, FOR GOODNESS' SAKE!!" St. Peter shouted, "It took me three months to find a priest up here! Do you have ANY idea how long it'll take me to find a lawyer?"

• • •

WIFE: I was an idiot when I married you 20 years ago ...
HUSBAND: Yes, dear, but I was blind with love and didn't notice.

• • •

Men's rules for women

These are our rules! Please note ... these are all numbered '1' ON PURPOSE!

1. Learn to work the toilet seat. You're a big girl. If it's up, put it down. We need it up, you need it down. You don't hear us complaining about you leaving it down.

1. Sunday = sports. It's like the full moon or the changing of the tides. Let it be.

1. Shopping is NOT a sport. And no, we are never going to think of it that way.

1. Ask for what you want. Let us be clear on this one: Subtle hints do not work! Strong hints do not work! Obvious hints do not work! Just say it!

1. "Yes" and "No" are perfectly acceptable answers to almost every question.

1. Come to us with a problem only if you want help solving it. That's what we do. Sympathy is what your girlfriends are for.

1. A headache that lasts for 17 months is a problem. See a doctor.

1. Anything we said 6 months ago is inadmissible in an argument. In fact, all comments become null and void after 7 days.

1. If you won't dress like the Victoria's Secret girls, don't expect us to act like soap opera guys.

1. If you think you're fat, you probably are. Don't ask us.

1. If something we said can be interpreted two ways, and one of the ways makes you sad or angry, we meant the other one.

1. You can either ask us to do something or tell us how you want it done. Not both. If you already know how best to do it, do it yourself.

1. Whenever possible, please say whatever you have to say during commercials.

1. Christopher Columbus did not need directions and neither do we.

1. ALL men see in only 16 colours, like Windows default settings. Peach, for example, is a fruit, not a colour. Pumpkin is also a fruit. We have no idea what mauve is.

1. If we ask what is wrong and you say "nothing," we will act like nothing's wrong. We know you are lying, but it is just not worth the hassle.
1. If you ask a question you don't want an answer to, expect an answer you don't want to hear.
1. When we have to go somewhere, absolutely anything you wear is fine. Really.
1. Don't ask us what we're thinking about unless you are prepared to discuss such topics as football, the shotgun rule, or monster trucks.
1. You have enough clothes.
1. You have too many shoes.
1. I am in shape. Round is a shape.
1. Thank you for reading this. Yes, I know I have to sleep on the couch tonight, but did you know men really don't mind that, it's like camping.

•••

Drive-through ATMs

THE NORMAL WAY
1. Drive up to cash machine
2. Wind down window
3. Insert card, enter your PIN
4. Enter amount of cash required and withdraw
5. Retrieve card, cash and receipt
6. Drive off

THE BLONDE WAY
1. Drive up to cash machine
2. Reverse a bit to align car window with machine
3. Restart stalled engine
4. Wind down window
5. Find handbag, dump all contents on to passenger seat to find card
6. Turn down radio
7. Attempt to insert card into machine

8. Open car door to allow easier access because car too far from machine
9. Insert card
10. Reinsert card right way up
11. Re-enter handbag to find diary with PIN on back page
12. Enter PIN
13. Press cancel and re-enter correct PIN
14. Enter amount of cash required
15. Check make up in rear-view mirror
16. Retrieve cash and receipt
17. Empty handbag again to locate purse and put cash inside
18. Place receipt in back of chequebook
19. Recheck make-up
20. Drive forward two metres
21. Reverse back to machine
22. Retrieve card
23. Empty handbag to find cardholder and replace card inside
24. Restart stalled engine and pull away
25. Drive two to three kilometres – release hand brake

•••

Random thoughts ...

▶ My mind not only wanders, it sometimes leaves completely.

▶ The best way to forget all your troubles is to wear tight shoes.

▶ Just when I was getting used to yesterday, along came today.

▶ Sometimes I think I understand everything, then I regain consciousness.

▶ They keep telling us to get in touch with our bodies. Mine isn't all that communicative but I heard from it the other day after I said, "Body, how'd you like to go to the six o'clock class in vigorous toning?" Clear as a bell, my body said, "Listen fatty ... do it and die."

Some people are just so cheap

A farmer and his wife went to a fair. The farmer was fascinated by the airplanes and asked a pilot how much a ride would cost. "R300 for 3 minutes," replied the pilot. "That's too much," said the farmer. The pilot thought for a second and then said, "I'll make you a deal. If you and your wife ride for 3 minutes without uttering a sound, the ride will be free. But if you make a sound, you'll have to pay R300."

The farmer and his wife agreed and went for a wild ride. After they landed, the pilot said to the farmer, "I want to congratulate you for not making a sound. You are a brave man."

"Maybe so," said the farmer, "But I gotta tell ya, I almost screamed when my wife fell out."

•••

A fairy told a married couple: "For being an exemplary married couple for 25 years, I will give you each a wish."

"I want to travel around the world with my dearest husband," said the wife. The fairy moved her magic wand and abracadabra! two tickets appeared on her hands. Now it was the husband's turn. He thought for a moment and said: "Well ... this moment is very romantic, but an opportunity like this only occurs once in a lifetime. So ... I'm sorry my love, but ... my wish is to have a wife 30 years younger than me." The wife was deeply disappointed but, a wish was a wish. The fairy made a circle with her magic wand and ... abracadabra! ... suddenly the husband was 90 years old.

•••

A keyring is a handy little gadget that allows you to lose all your keys at once.

What we've learned from the movies

Imagine you lived a remote life but had satellite television and were able to see movies all of the time. How misguided would your life be? Below are a few of the things that you would have learned.

1. All beds have special L-shaped cover sheets which reach up to armpit level on a woman but only to waist level on the man lying beside her.
2. If being chased through town, you can usually take cover in a passing St. Patrick's Day parade – at any time of the year.
3. All grocery shopping bags contain at least one stick of French bread.
4. Once applied, lipstick will never rub off – even while scuba diving.
5. During all police investigations it will be necessary to visit a strip club at least once.
6. The Eiffel tower can be seen from any window in Paris.
7. Should you wish to pass yourself off as a German officer, it will not be necessary to speak the language. A German accent will do.
8. Most laptop computers are powerful enough to override the communication systems of any invading alien civilization.
9. If staying in a haunted house, women should investigate any strange noises in their most revealing underwear.
10. It is always possible to park directly outside the building you are visiting.
11. All bombs are fitted with electronic timing devices with large red readouts so you know exactly when they're going to go off.
12. When they are alone, all non-native English speakers prefer to speak English to each other.
13. When paying for a taxi, don't look at your wallet as you take out a bill – just grab one at random and hand it over. It will always be the exact fare.
14. A man will show no pain while taking the most ferocious beating but will wince when a woman tries to clean his wounds.

•••

CONTINUING EDUCATION FOR WOMEN

Training courses are now available for women on the following subjects:

1. Silence, the Final Frontier: Where no woman has gone before

2. The undiscovered side of banking: Making deposits

3. Parties: Going without new outfits

4. Man management: Minor household chores can wait till after the game

5. Bathroom etiquette I: Men need space in the bathroom cabinet too

6. Bathroom etiquette II: His razor is his

7. Communication skills I: Tears – the last resort, not the first

8. Communication skills II: Thinking before speaking

9. Communication skills III: Getting what you want without nagging

10. Driving a car safely: A skill you CAN acquire

11. Telephone skills: How to hang up

12. Introduction to parking

13. Advanced parking: Reversing into a space

14. Compliments: Accepting them gracefully

15. Dancing: Why men don't like to

16. Classic clothing: Wearing outfits you already have

17. Household dust: A harmless natural occurrence only women notice

18. Integrating your laundry: Washing it all together

19. Oil and gas: Your car needs both

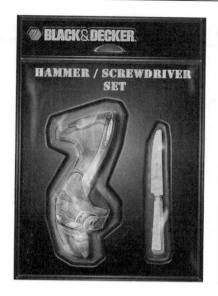

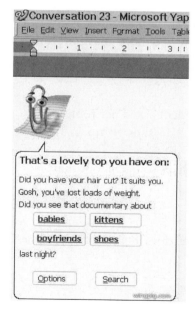

Why men shouldn't take messages

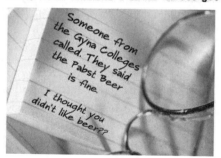

Men and horses

A man is sitting quietly reading his paper when his wife sneaks up behind him and whacks him on the head with a frying pan.

"What was that for?" he says.

"That was for the piece of paper in your pocket with the name Mary Lou written on it," she replies.

"Two weeks ago when I went to Bay Meadows, Mary Lou was the name of one of the horses I bet on," he explains. She looks satisfied, apologizes, and goes back to what she was doing.

Three days later he's again sitting in his chair reading, when she nails him with an even bigger frying pan, knocking him out cold. When he comes to, he says, "What on earth was THAT for?"

"Your horse phoned."

• • •

A newly-married man asked his wife, "Would you have married me if my father hadn't left me a fortune?"

"Honey," the woman replied sweetly, "I'd have married you no matter who left you a fortune."

• • •

"How was your blind date?" a college student asked her roommate.

"Terrible!" the roommate answered. "He showed up in his 1932 Rolls Royce."

"Wow! That's a very expensive car. What's so bad about that?"

"He's the original owner."

• • •

How many intelligent, sensitive, caring men does it take to do the dishes? Answer: Both of them.

• • •

First husband (proudly): "My wife's an angel!"
Second husband: "You're lucky. Mine's still alive."

Any closet is a walk-in closet if you try hard enough.

Marriage is the triumph of imagination over intelligence.
A second marriage is the triumph of hope over experience.

•••

Interviewer to millionaire: "To whom do you owe your success as a millionaire?"

Millionaire: "I owe everything to my wife."

Interviewer: "Wow, she must be some woman. What were you before you married her?"

Millionaire: "A billionaire."

•••

Quotes on marriage

"My wife and I were happy for twenty years. Then we met."
— Rodney Dangerfield

"A married man should forget his mistakes; no use two people remembering the same thing."
— Duane Dewel

"Eighty percent of married men cheat in America. The rest cheat in Europe."
— Jackie Mason

"I don't think I'll get married again. I'll just find a woman I don't like and give her a house."
— Lewis Grizzard

"The difference between divorce and legal separation is that legal separation gives a husband time to hide his money."
— Johnny Carson

The not-so-dumb blonde

A blonde and a lawyer are seated next to each other on a flight from Johannesburg to Cape Town. The lawyer asks if she would like to play a fun game.

The blonde, tired, just wants to nap, so she politely declines and rolls over to the window to catch a few winks. The lawyer persists, and explains that the game is easy and a lot of fun. He says, "I'll ask you a question. If you don't know the answer, you pay me R10, and vice versa."

Again she declines and tries to get some sleep. The lawyer, now agitated, says, "Okay, if you don't know the answer, you pay me R10, and if I don't know the answer, I'll pay you R1 000." This catches the blonde's attention and, figuring there will be no end to this torment, agrees to the game.

The lawyer asks the first question: "What's the distance from the earth to the moon?"

The blonde doesn't say a word, reaches into her purse, pulls out a R10 note, and hands it to the lawyer.

"Okay," says the lawyer, "your turn."

She asks, "What goes up a hill with three legs and comes down with four legs?"

The lawyer, puzzled, takes out his laptop computer and searches all his references ... no answer. He taps into the air phone with his modem and searches the Internet and the National Library ... no answer. Frustrated, he sends e-mails to all his friends and co-workers, but to no avail.

After an hour, he wakes the blonde and hands her R1 000. The blonde thanks him and turns back to get more sleep. The lawyer, who is more than a little irked, stirs the blonde and asks, "Well, what's the answer?"

Without a word, the blonde reaches into her purse, hands the lawyer R10, and goes back to sleep.

• • •

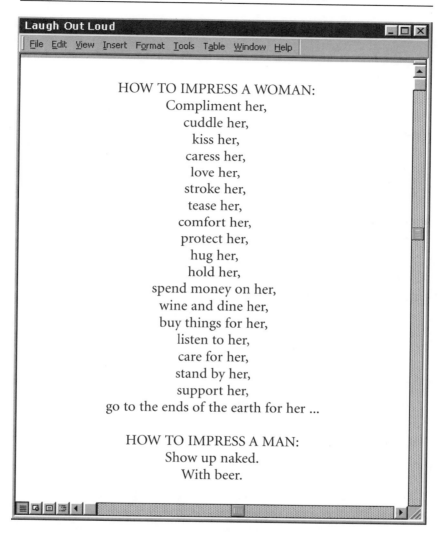

Laugh Out Loud _ □ X

File Edit View Insert Format Tools Table Window Help

HOW TO IMPRESS A WOMAN:
Compliment her,
cuddle her,
kiss her,
caress her,
love her,
stroke her,
tease her,
comfort her,
protect her,
hug her,
hold her,
spend money on her,
wine and dine her,
buy things for her,
listen to her,
care for her,
stand by her,
support her,
go to the ends of the earth for her ...

HOW TO IMPRESS A MAN:
Show up naked.
With beer.

•••

I still miss my ex-husband ... but my aim is improving.

•••

It was a stifling hot day and a man fainted in the middle of a busy intersection.

Traffic quickly piled up in all directions while a woman rushed to help him. When she knelt down to loosen his collar, a man emerged from the crowd, pushed her aside and said, "It's all right, honey, I've had a course in first aid."

The woman stood up and watched as he took the ill man's pulse and prepared to administer artificial respiration. At this point she tapped him on the shoulder and said, "When you get to the part about calling a doctor, I'm already here."

•••

A man and his wife were having some problems at home and were giving each other the silent treatment.

The next week, the man realized that he would need his wife to wake him at 5 am for a flight to Europe. Not wanting to be the first to break the silence, he finally wrote on a piece of paper, "Please wake me tomorrow morning at 5 am." The next morning the man woke up only to discover it was 9 am, and that he had missed his flight.

Furious, he was about to go and see why his wife hadn't woken him when he noticed a piece of paper by the bed – it said: "It's 5 am. Wake up."

•••

Two men were having an awfully slow round of golf because the two women in front of them managed to get into every sand trap, lake and rough on the course. They didn't bother to wave the men on through, which is proper golf etiquette.

After two hours of waiting and waiting, one man said, "I think I'll walk up there and ask those ladies to let us play through." He walked out on to the fairway, got halfway to the women, stopped, turned around and came back, explaining, "I can't do it. One of those women is my wife and the other is my mistress! Maybe you'd better go talk to them."

The second man walked towards the women, got halfway there and, just as his partner had done, stopped, turned around, walked back and said: "Small world."

•••

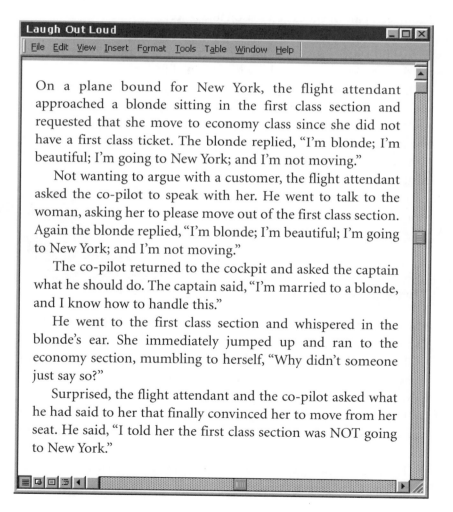

Laugh Out Loud

File Edit View Insert Format Tools Table Window Help

On a plane bound for New York, the flight attendant approached a blonde sitting in the first class section and requested that she move to economy class since she did not have a first class ticket. The blonde replied, "I'm blonde; I'm beautiful; I'm going to New York; and I'm not moving."

Not wanting to argue with a customer, the flight attendant asked the co-pilot to speak with her. He went to talk to the woman, asking her to please move out of the first class section. Again the blonde replied, "I'm blonde; I'm beautiful; I'm going to New York; and I'm not moving."

The co-pilot returned to the cockpit and asked the captain what he should do. The captain said, "I'm married to a blonde, and I know how to handle this."

He went to the first class section and whispered in the blonde's ear. She immediately jumped up and ran to the economy section, mumbling to herself, "Why didn't someone just say so?"

Surprised, the flight attendant and the co-pilot asked what he had said to her that finally convinced her to move from her seat. He said, "I told her the first class section was NOT going to New York."

A blonde and the alligator shoes

A young blonde was on vacation in the depths of Louisiana. She wanted a pair of genuine alligator shoes, but was very reluctant to pay the high prices the local vendors were asking. After becoming very frustrated with the 'no haggle' attitude of one of the shopkeepers, the blonde shouted, "Maybe I'll just go out and catch my own alligator so I can get a pair of shoes at a reasonable price!"

The shopkeeper said, "By all means, be my guest. Maybe you'll get lucky and catch yourself a big one!" Determined, the blonde headed for the swamps, set on catching herself an alligator.

Later that day, the shopkeeper was driving home when he spotted the young woman standing waist deep in the water, shotgun in hand. Just then, he saw a huge 9-foot alligator swimming quickly towards her. She took aim, killed the creature and with a great deal of effort, hauled it on to the swamp bank. Laying nearby were several more of the dead creatures.

The shopkeeper watched in amazement. Just then the blonde flipped the alligator on its back and, frustrated, shouted out, "Damn it! This one isn't wearing any shoes either!"

●●●

Three blonde guys

Three blonde guys are stranded on one side of a wide river and don't know how to get across.

The first blonde guy wishes he is smart enough to think of a way to cross the river. Poof! His wish is granted and he turns into a brown-haired man and he swims across.

The second blonde guy wishes that he can think of a better way to cross the river. Poof! His wish is granted and he turns into a red-haired man and he builds a boat and rows across.

The third blonde guy wishes that he could be the smartest of all and POOF! he turns into a woman and walks across the bridge.

●●●

106

• • •

Two blondes are walking down the street. One notices a compact on the sidewalk and leans down to pick it up. She opens it, looks in the mirror and says, "Hmm, this person looks familiar." The second blonde says, "Here, let me see!" So the first blonde hands her the compact. The second one looks in the mirror and says, "You dummy, it's me!"

• • •

Two bowling teams, one all blondes and one all brunettes, charter a double-decker bus for a weekend bowling tournament. The brunette team rides in the bottom of the bus. The blonde team rides on the upper deck.

The brunette team down below is having a great time, when one of them realises she doesn't hear anything from the blondes upstairs. She decides to go up and investigate. When the brunette reaches the top, she finds all the blondes frozen in fear, staring straight ahead at the road and clutching the seats in front of them with white knuckles. She says, "What the heck's going on up here? We're having a grand time downstairs!"

One of the blondes looks up and says, "Yeah, well, you've got a driver!!!!"

• • •

A married couple were asleep when the phone rang at two in the morning. The wife picked up the phone, listened a moment and said, "How should I know? That's 200 kilometres from here!" and hung up. The husband asked, "Who was that?"

The wife replied, "I don't know; some woman wanting to know 'if the coast is clear'."

• • •

Today's subliminal message:

A blonde was down on her luck. In order to raise some money, she decided to kidnap a kid and hold him for ransom. She went to the playground, grabbed a kid, took him behind a tree and told him, "I've kidnapped you."

She then wrote a note saying, "I've kidnapped your kid. Tomorrow morning, put R100 000 in a paper bag and leave it under the pecan tree next to the slide on the north side of the playground." – Signed, A Blonde.

The blonde then pinned the note to the kid's shirt and sent him home to show it to his parents. The next morning the blonde checked, and sure enough, a paper bag was sitting beneath the pecan tree. The blonde opened the bag and found the R100 000 with a note that said, "How could you do this to a fellow blonde?"

•••

There were two blonde guys working for the city council. One would dig a hole, the other would follow behind him and fill the hole in. They worked furiously all day without rest, one guy digging a hole, the other guy filling it in again. An onlooker was amazed at their hard work, but couldn't understand what they were doing. So he asked the hole digger, "Appreciate the effort you are putting into your work, but what's the story? You dig a hole and your partner follows behind and fills it up again." The hole digger wiped his brow and sighed, "Well, normally we are a three-man team, but the guy who plants the trees is sick today."

•••

A blonde suspects her boyfriend of cheating on her, so she goes out and buys a gun. She goes to his apartment unexpectedly and when she opens the door she finds him in the arms of a redhead. Well, the blonde is really angry. She opens her purse to take out the gun, and as she does so, she is overcome with grief. She takes the gun and puts it to her head. The boyfriend yells, "No, honey, don't do it!" The blonde replies, "Shut up, you're next!"

•••

God may have made man first, but there is always a rough draft before a final copy.

•••

There's this blonde out for a walk. She comes to a river and sees another blonde on the opposite bank. "Yoo-hoo!" she shouts, "How can I get to the other side?" The second blonde looks up the river then down the river and shouts back, "You ARE on the other side!"

•••

Final exam

The blonde surfer reported for his final university examination that consisted of yes/no type questions.

He took his seat in the examination hall, stared at the question paper for about five minutes and then, in a fit of inspiration, took out his wallet, removed a coin and started tossing it, marking the answer sheet "Yes" for Heads and "No" for Tails.

Within half an hour he was all done, while the rest of the class were still sweating it out.

During the last few minutes he was seen desperately throwing the coin again, muttering and sweating. The moderator, alarmed, approached him and asked what was going on.

"I finished the exam in half an hour," he said, "but now I'm trying to check my answers."

•••

Husband and cat lost ... reward for cat.

I feel like I'm diagonally parked in a parallel universe.

Connect the DOTS!

1. ●

2. ●

Get through the MAZE!

Start

Finish

See if you can find your way through
this perplexing maze.

One of these is a square
and one is not.
Which one is the square?

A

B

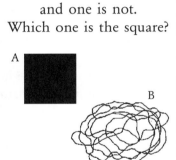

The artist who drew this picture has
cleverly left out a part of this drawing.
Can you guess what this animal is by
examining the incomplete drawing?

Then see if you can complete the drawing.
This animal is a _____.

Find the elephant

Can you find the elephant
hidden in this picture?

Tic Tac Toe challenge

You are battling for the Tic Tac Toe
Championship of the World. You
have the last move and one open
square is left. You are X. Good luck!

X	O	X
O		O
X	O	X

• • •

Two blondes decide to go duck hunting. Neither one of them has ever been duck hunting before and after several hours they still haven't bagged any.

One hunter looks at the other and says, "I just don't understand it – why aren't we getting any ducks?"

Her friend says, "I keep telling you, I don't think we're throwing the dog high enough."

• • •

She was so blonde that ...

▸ She thought a quarterback was a refund.

▸ At the bottom of the application form where it said "Sign here", she put Sagittarius.

▸ If she spoke her mind, she'd be speechless.

▸ When she heard that 90% of all crimes were committed around the home, she moved.

▸ It took her months to figure out she could use her AM radio at night.

▸ She was staring at the frozen orange juice because it said "concentrate".

▸ She thinks Taco Bell is a Mexican phone company.

▸ She told me to meet her at the corner of WALK and DON'T WALK.

▸ When she was on the highway going to the airport and saw a sign that said "Airport Left", she turned around and went home.

▸ She studied for a blood test and failed.

▸ She looked into a box of Fruit Loops and said, "Oh, look! Doughnut seeds!"

Those poor blondes

How did the blonde break her leg raking leaves?
... She fell out of the tree.

How did the blonde die drinking milk?
... The cow stepped on her.

What do you call 4 blondes in a Volkswagen?
... Far-from-thinkin'.

Why can't blondes put in light bulbs?
... They keep breaking them with the hammer.

Did you hear about the blonde who shot an arrow into the air?
... She missed.

What do you call it when a blonde blows into another blonde's ear?
... Data transfer.

What did the blonde say when she found out she was pregnant?
... "I wonder if it's mine?"

Why shouldn't blondes have coffee breaks?
... It takes too long to retrain them.

What do you call an eternity?
... Four blondes at a four-way stop.

What goes "Brrrrm. Screech. Brrrrm. Screech. Brrrrm. Screech."?
... A blonde at a flashing red robot.

•••

Two blondes are walking along the beach. The one says to the other, "Oh look, there's a dead seagull." The other blonde looks up and says, "Where?"

Ageing
and
Health

One out of every four people is suffering from some form of
mental illness. Check three friends. If they're OK, then it's you.

The problem with ageing

Two elderly couples were enjoying friendly conversation when one of the men asked the other, "Fred, how was the memory clinic you went to last month?"

"Outstanding," Fred replied. "They taught us all the latest psychological techniques – visualization, association – it made a huge difference for me."

"That's great! What was the name of the clinic?"

Fred went blank. He thought and thought, but couldn't remember. Then a smile broke across his face and he asked, "What do you call that red flower with the long stem and thorns?"

"You mean a rose?"

"Yes, that's it!" He turned to his wife ... "Rose, what was the name of that clinic?"

•••

Two elderly women were out driving in a big automatic and both could barely see over the dashboard. They came to a traffic light. It was red. They sailed through. The woman in the passenger seat thought to herself, "I must be losing it. I could have sworn we just went through a red light."

Later, another red light – again they went right through. This time the woman in the passenger seat was sure the light had been red but was really concerned that she might be losing it. She paid very close attention to the next lights. They were definitely red – and the car sailed through. She said, "Mildred, you've shot three red lights in a row! You could have killed us!"

Mildred sat bolt upright and said, "Good gracious! Am *I* driving?"

•••

I'm not suddenly a Dirty Old Man ...
I've been practising since 1943.

114

The hardest years in life are those between ten and seventy.
– Helen Hayes (at 73)

Old age ain't no place for sissies.
– Bette Davis

You know you're growing older when ...

1. Everything hurts, and what doesn't hurt doesn't work.
2. You feel like the morning after the night before, and you haven't been anywhere.
3. Your little black book contains only names ending in M.D.
4. You get winded playing chess.
5. A dripping tap causes an uncontrollable bladder urge.
6. You know all the answers, but nobody asks you the questions.
7. You look forward to a dull evening.
8. You turn out the lights for economic rather than romantic reasons.
9. You sit in a rocking chair and can't get it going.
10. Your idea of a night out is sitting on the patio.
11. Your knees buckle but your belt won't.
12. You and your teeth don't sleep together.
13. Your back goes out more often than you do.
14. The little grey-haired lady you help across the street is your wife.
15. You have too much room in the house and not enough in the medicine cabinet.
16. You sit down at the breakfast table and hear "Snap! Crackle! Pop!" and you're not eating cereal.
17. You sink your teeth into a steak ... and they stay there.

• • •

Madness takes its toll. Please have exact change.

I'm not 50 – I'm 18 with 32 years experience.

• • •

Three sisters aged 92, 94 and 96 lived in a house together. One night, the 96-year-old drew a bath. She put her foot in and paused. She yelled to the other sisters, "Was I getting in or out of the bath?"

The 94-year-old yelled back, "I don't know. I'll come up and see." She started up the stairs and paused. "Was I going up the stairs or down?"

The 92-year-old was sitting at the kitchen table having tea and listening to her sisters. She shook her head and said, "I sure hope I never get that forgetful." She knocked on wood for good measure. Then she yelled, "I'll come up and help both of you as soon as I see who's at the door!"

• • •

Two elderly ladies had been friends for many decades. Over the years they had shared all kinds of activities and adventures. Lately, their activities had been limited to meeting a few times a week to play cards.

One day, as they were playing cards, one looked at the other and said, "Now don't get mad at me. I know we've been friends for a long time, but I just can't think of your name! I've thought and thought, but I can't remember it. Please tell me what your name is."

For at least three minutes her friend just sat and glared at her.

Finally she said, "How soon do you need to know?"

• • •

The older a man gets, the further he had to walk
to school as a boy.
– DCA

Age is relative

Age is just "relative" or another "relativity". Do you realize that the only time in our lives when we like to get old is when we're kids? If you're less than 10 years old, you're so excited about ageing that you think in fractions.

How old are you? ... "I'm four and a half" ... You're never 36 and a half ... you're four and a half going on five! That's the key. You get into your teens, now they can't hold you back. You jump to the next number. How old are you? "I'm gonna be 16." You could be 12, but you're gonna be 16. And then the greatest day of your life happens ... you become 21. Even the words sound like a ceremony ... you BECOME 21 ... YES!!!

But then you turn 30 ... oohhh what happened there? Makes you sound like bad milk ... He TURNED, we had to throw him out. There's no fun now. What's wrong?? What changed? You BECOME 21, you TURN 30, then you're PUSHING 40 ... stay over there, it's all slipping away.

You BECOME 21, you TURN 30, you're PUSHING 40, you REACH 50 and your dreams are gone. Then you MAKE IT to 60 ... you didn't think you'd make it!

So you BECOME 21, you TURN 30, you're PUSHING 40, you REACH 50, you MAKE IT to 60 ... then you build up so much speed you HIT 70!

After that, it's a day by day thing. After that, you HIT Wednesday. You get into your 80s, you HIT lunch. You HIT 4:30! My grandmother won't even buy green bananas. It's an investment you know, and maybe a bad one.

And it doesn't end there ... into the 90s you start going backwards ... I was JUST 92 ... Then a strange thing happens. If you make it over 100, you become a little kid again ... "I'm 100 and a half!!!!"

– George Carlin

•••

The little old couple

A little old couple walked into a McDonald's one cold winter evening.

The old man walked up to the cash register, placed his order and paid for their meal. They then took a table near the back wall and started taking food off the tray.

There was just one hamburger, one packet of French fries and one drink. The little old man unwrapped the plain hamburger and cut it in half.

He placed one half in front of the little old lady. Then he carefully counted out the French fries, divided them into two piles and neatly placed one pile in front of her.

He took a sip of the drink, then she took a sip. He started to eat his few bites while she sat watching him.

A young man seeing this, thought, "That poor old couple!" So he went over to their table and politely offered to buy them another meal. The old man replied that they were just fine. They were used to sharing everything. The old man continued to eat while the little old lady just stared at him.

The young man, noticing that the little old lady still hadn't eaten a thing, came over again and begged them to let him buy them something. This time it was the old lady's turn to say no, thank you, they were used to sharing everything.

As the little old man finished eating and was wiping his face with a napkin, the young man could stand it no longer and asked, "Ma'am, what's wrong then? If you share everything, why aren't you eating?"

"I'm waiting for the teeth," she replied.

• • •

I'm not a complete idiot – several parts are missing.

Sometimes I wake up grumpy. Other times I let her sleep.

•••

As a senior citizen was driving down the highway, his car phone rang. Answering, he heard his wife's voice urgently warning him, "Herman, I just heard on the news that there's a car going the wrong way on the N1. Please be careful!"

"Hell," said Herman, "It's not just ONE car. It's HUNDREDS of them!"

•••

Best exercise advice in a long time

Q: I've heard that cardiovascular exercise can prolong life. Is this true?

A: Your heart is only good for so many beats, and that's it ... don't waste them on exercise. Everything wears out eventually. Speeding up your heart will not make you live longer; that's like saying you can extend the life of your car by driving it faster. Want to live longer? Take a nap.

Q: Should I cut down on meat and eat more fruits and vegetables?

A: You must grasp logistical efficiencies. What does a cow eat? Hay and corn. And what are these? Vegetables. So a steak is nothing more than an efficient mechanism of delivering vegetables to your system. Need grain? Eat chicken. Beef is also a good source of field grass (green leafy vegetable). And a pork chop can give you 100% of your recommended daily allowance of vegetable products.

Q: How can I calculate my body/fat ratio?

A: Well, if you have a body, and you have body fat, your ratio is one to one. If you have two bodies, your ratio is two to one, etc.

Q: What are some of the advantages of participating in a regular exercise program?

A: Can't think of a single one, sorry. My philosophy is: No Pain ... Good.

Q: Aren't fried foods bad for you?

A: You're not listening. Foods are fried these days in vegetable oil. In fact, they're permeated in it. How could getting more vegetables be bad for you?

Q: What's the secret to healthy eating?

A: Thicker gravy.

Q: Will sit-ups help prevent me from getting soft around the middle?

A: Definitely not! When you exercise a muscle, it gets bigger. You should only be doing sit-ups if you want a bigger stomach.

Q: Is chocolate bad for me?

A: Are you crazy? HELLO! ... Cocoa beans ... another vegetable!!! It's the best feel-good food around!

Well, I hope this has cleared up any misconceptions you may have had about food and diets. Now go have a cookie ... flour is a veggie!

• • •

Stress is when you wake up screaming and you realize you haven't fallen asleep yet.

I have flabby thighs, but fortunately my stomach covers them.

If God wanted me to touch my toes, he'd have put them on my knees.

If swimming is good for your figure, explain whales to me.
– Steven Wright

Brain over – Insert coin

What is red and invisible? No tomatoes.

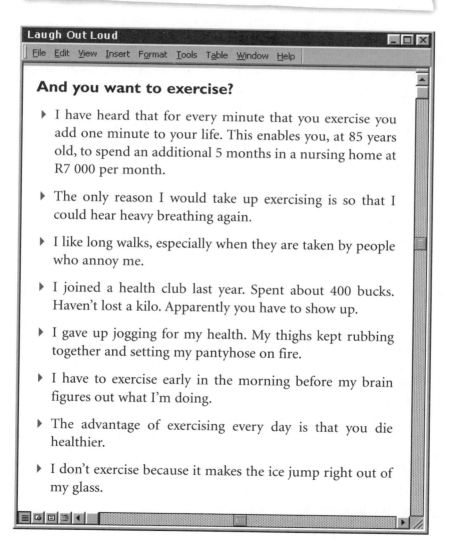

Laugh Out Loud — □ ×

File   Edit   View   Insert   Format   Tools   Table   Window   Help

And you want to exercise?

▸ I have heard that for every minute that you exercise you add one minute to your life. This enables you, at 85 years old, to spend an additional 5 months in a nursing home at R7 000 per month.

▸ The only reason I would take up exercising is so that I could hear heavy breathing again.

▸ I like long walks, especially when they are taken by people who annoy me.

▸ I joined a health club last year. Spent about 400 bucks. Haven't lost a kilo. Apparently you have to show up.

▸ I gave up jogging for my health. My thighs kept rubbing together and setting my pantyhose on fire.

▸ I have to exercise early in the morning before my brain figures out what I'm doing.

▸ The advantage of exercising every day is that you die healthier.

▸ I don't exercise because it makes the ice jump right out of my glass.

Making that annual trip to the gym

Four years ago, in a fit of fitness mania, I took out a membership contract with a popular health club chain. It's a great arrangement, and it works like this. Every month I pay them R95, and then I don't go to the gym. The contract is for life – as long as I keep paying, I can continue to not go to the gym until the day I die. And I'm not just failing to go to the gym in Claremont, where I originally signed up. No siree, this is a multi-access membership – there is a whole string of gyms, some very close to where I work, that I can conveniently avoid going to every day. If I had to move to another city, say, Johannesburg, I could cheerfully not get around to going to franchised gyms there.

My membership can even be used in London. With the current exchange rate, paying R95 not to go to a gym in London will only cost me about £7. What a saving!

Of course, there was a time when I did go. I was in there, lifting, pulling and pushing for all I was worth, for at least two weeks after I got my membership card. Keen not to overtrain (didn't want to accidentally wind up built like Arnold Schwarzewhatever), I devised a roster that would ensure I went to the gym three times a week.

But then we went through a really busy time at work, I got that persistent bout of 'flu, and I tired of the pain involved in moving lumps of metal away from the ground where they preferred to be. Recently, I realized I hadn't seen the inside of a gym for more than a year and a fitness zeal swept over me. Digging my forgotten gym bag out from the back of my cupboard, I set off to the club with a 'Terminator' look in my eye.

It was a bit embarrassing, struggling to unstick my membership card from my leather wallet, to which it had heat-sealed itself, while the blonde at reception gave me a knowing look before scanning the barcode. Deep in a computer database somewhere, emergency software sprang into action. Analysing the printout, two yuppies in padded suits glanced at each other. "O'Reilly's gone active," said the one. "And he's been a sleeper for over a year."

"Strange," replied the other. "Still, it won't last."

I was careful to go on a weekday morning, when it was nice and quiet. But no matter how empty it is, there is always one bulging guy there, wearing wrist-guards, a don't-rupture-yourself leather belt and one of those vests with loops so big he might as well just pull on an apron and be done with it. I call him 'Mr Iscor' because he can be counted upon to have a day's worth of steel mill production in each hand at any time. He's not there for fun – he's paid by the gym to be there to humble those of us who can't bench-press our own weight.

Now, there are two ways to go about a first-visit-in-ages gym session. You can either go steroidal, throw around the biggest weights you can move, and then have your doctor book you off work for two days because you can't move. Or you can ease into it by doing the 'recovering from injury' drill.

It's a wheeze I've perfected. Work out with light weights, and then occasionally grab a muscle and get a faraway look in your eyes as if you're tuning in to damaged fibrils. People will spot you and say, "Ah, he's using light weights because he's recovering from some wrenching injury," and your manly pride will remain unscathed.

Halfway through my lightweight non-workout, I arrived at the bench-press machine – and ran straight into Mr Iscor.

"You want to alternate with me?" he said in a 'don't refuse' voice.

My mind was screaming "Run!" but I heard my mouth saying "Yeah, sure."

"Good, we'll train together!" he said, loading enough metal on the machine to make a small car. "You go first!"

I'll show you, Mr Babyfat, I said to myself.

When I struggled out of bed the next morning, my arms were so stiff I couldn't brush my teeth. And I had to type using my nose. But the best part is, I worked out that the session only cost me R1140. In fact, it felt so good to be back in training, I've decided I'm going to go next year as well. Look out, Arnold!

– Michael O'Reilly
  Condensed from the *Cape Times* (July 9, 1996)

•••

123

Medical terms you should know ...

Artery	The study of paintings
Bacteria	Back door of the cafeteria
Barium	What you do with dead patients
Bowels	A E I O U
Caesarian section	A suburb in Rome
Cat scan	A search for kitty
Cauterize	Making eye contact with the nurse
Colic	A sheep dog
D & C	Where Washington is
Dilate	To live longer
Enema	Not your friend
Fester	Quicker
Genital	Not a Jew
Impotent	Distinguished and well-known
Labour pains	Getting hurt at work
Medical staff	Doctor's walking stick
Morbid	Higher offer
Nitrates	Cheaper than day rates
Node	Was aware of
Outpatient	A person who's fainted
Pap smear	A fatherhood test
Pelvis	A cousin of Elvis
Post-operative	A letter courier
Recovery room	A place where you do upholstery
Rectum	Damn nearly killed him
Sciatic	An attic with a view
Seizure	The Roman Emperor
Tablet	A small table
Terminal illness	When you get sick at the airport
Tumour	More than one people
Urine	The opposite of "you're out"
Varicose	Close by
Vein	Conceited

Interviewing crazy

A man who had been in a mental home for some years finally seemed to have improved to the point where it was thought he might be released.

The head of the institution, in a fit of commendable caution, decided, however, to interview him first.

"Tell me," he said, "if we release you, as we are considering doing, what do you intend to do with your life?"

The inmate said, "It would be wonderful to get back to real life and, if I do, I will certainly refrain from making my former mistake. I was a nuclear physicist, you know, and it was the stress of my work in weapons research that helped put me here. If I am released, I shall confine myself to work in pure theory, where I trust the situation will be less difficult and stressful."

"Marvellous," said the head of the institution.

"Or else," ruminated the inmate, "I might teach. There is something to be said for spending one's life in bringing up a new generation of scientists."

"Absolutely," said the head.

"Then again, I might write. There is considerable need for books on science for the general public. Or I might even write a novel based on my experiences in this fine institution."

"An interesting possibility," said the head.

"And finally, if none of these things appeals to me, I can always continue to be a teakettle."

•••

Allow me to introduce my selves.

Do not disturb. Already disturbed!

Out of my mind. Back in five minutes.

Messages for the unstable

"Hello, and welcome to the mental health hotline.

– If you are obsessive-compulsive, press 1 repeatedly.

– If you are co-dependent, please ask someone to press 2 for you.

– If you have multiple personalities, press 3, 4, 5 and 6.

– If you are paranoid, we know who you are and what you want. Stay on the line so we can trace your call.

– If you are delusional, press 7 and your call will be transferred to the mother ship.

– If you are schizophrenic, listen carefully and a small voice will tell you which number to press.

– If you are a manic-depressive, it doesn't matter which number you press – no one will answer.

– If you are dyslexic, press 9696969696969.

– If you have a nervous disorder, please fidget with the hash key until a representative comes on the line.

– If you have amnesia, press 8 and state your name, address, phone number, date of birth, social security number and your mother's maiden name.

– If you have post-traumatic stress disorder, slowly and carefully press 000.

– If you have bipolar disorder, please leave a message after the beep or before the beep. Or after the beep. Please wait for the beep.

– If you have short-term memory loss, press 9.

– If you have short-term memory loss, press 9.

– If you have short-term memory loss, press 9.

– If you have short-term memory loss, press 9.

– If you have low self-esteem, please hang up. All our operators are too busy to talk to you."

•••

A Freudian slip is when you say one thing but mean your mother.

A psychiatric hospital

After hearing that one of the patients in a psychiatric hospital had saved another from a suicide attempt by pulling him out of a bathtub, the hospital director reviewed the rescuer's file and called him into his office.

"Mr Haroldson, your records and your heroic behaviour indicate that you're ready to go home. I'm only sorry that the man you saved later killed himself with a rope around the neck."

"Oh, he didn't kill himself," Mr Haroldson replied, "I hung him up to dry."

• • •

Everyone thinks I'm psychotic, except for my friends deep inside the earth.

On a tombstone: "I TOLD YOU I WAS SICK!"

You're just jealous because the voices only talk to me.

I'm not crazy, I've just been in a very bad mood for 30 years.

• • •

When the new patient was settled comfortably on the couch, the psychiatrist began his therapy session. "I'm not aware of your problem," the doctor said, "so perhaps you should start at the very beginning."

"Of course," replied the patient. "In the beginning, I created the Heavens and the Earth ..."

Daily affirmations for the unstable

✓ I no longer need to punish, deceive or compromise myself. Unless, of course, I want to stay employed.

✓ A good scapegoat is nearly as welcome as a solution to the problem.

✓ As I let go of my feelings of guilt, I can get in touch with my inner sociopath.

✓ I have the power to channel my imagination into ever-soaring levels of suspicion and paranoia.

✓ Today, I will gladly share my experience and advice, for there are no sweeter words than "I told you so."

✓ I need not suffer in silence while I can still moan, whimper and complain.

✓ I assume full responsibility for my actions, except the ones that are someone else's fault.

✓ I honour my personality flaws, for without them I would have no personality at all.

✓ Joan of Arc heard voices too.

✓ Why should I waste my time reliving the past when I can spend it worrying about the future?

✓ Who can I blame for my own problems? Just give me a minute ... I'll find someone.

✓ As I learn to trust the universe, I no longer need to carry a gun.

✓ I will find humour in my everyday life by looking for people I can laugh at.

✓ I am willing to make the mistakes if someone else is willing to learn from them.

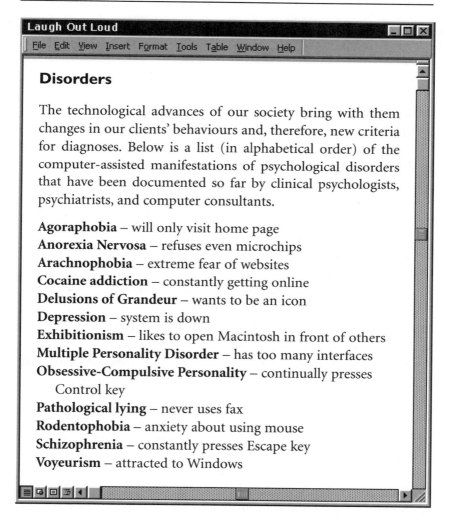

Laugh Out Loud

File   Edit   View   Insert   Format   Tools   Table   Window   Help

Disorders

The technological advances of our society bring with them changes in our clients' behaviours and, therefore, new criteria for diagnoses. Below is a list (in alphabetical order) of the computer-assisted manifestations of psychological disorders that have been documented so far by clinical psychologists, psychiatrists, and computer consultants.

Agoraphobia – will only visit home page
Anorexia Nervosa – refuses even microchips
Arachnophobia – extreme fear of websites
Cocaine addiction – constantly getting online
Delusions of Grandeur – wants to be an icon
Depression – system is down
Exhibitionism – likes to open Macintosh in front of others
Multiple Personality Disorder – has too many interfaces
Obsessive-Compulsive Personality – continually presses Control key
Pathological lying – never uses fax
Rodentophobia – anxiety about using mouse
Schizophrenia – constantly presses Escape key
Voyeurism – attracted to Windows

• • •

I don't suffer from insanity. I enjoy every minute of it.

A handkerchief allows you to put into your pocket what you don't want in your nose.

Psychoanalysis finally explained

Psychoanalysis, which is easier to understand than to spell, tells us what we really think when we think we think a thing. Without psychoanalysis we should never know that when we think a thing, the thing we think is not the thing we think we think, but only the thing that makes us think the thing we think we think.

It is all a question of the Unconscious. The Unconscious enables us to think we are thinking about the thing we think we want to think about, while all the time the thing we really want to think about is being thought about unconsciously by the Unconscious.

The Unconscious is a survival from our barbaric ancestry and has no manners.

As the sort of thing the Unconscious thinks about is not the sort of thing we care to think we think about, the Unconscious takes care not to let us think it is thinking about what is thinking about. If we are in any danger of thinking we are thinking what we are really thinking about, the thing we are thinking about is sublimated into something we don't mind thinking we are thinking about.

Actually the Unconscious is divided into two parts: the part that thinks the thing, and the part that prevents our thinking we are thinking the thing. This preventing of our thinking we are thinking the thing we do not care to think we are thinking is called Repression.

Repression is due to the Superego, which is very genteel.

There is friction between the Superego and coarse part of the Unconscious, or the Id. The Id thinks a thing which the Superego thinks it ought not to think, and the Superego represses the thing the Id thinks so that we never think we think it. But unless the Id thinks we are thinking it, the Id becomes dissatisfied and causes trouble.

As, whatever the Id thinks, we can only think we are thinking the sort of thing the Superego thinks we ought to think, we have to make the Id think we are thinking the thing the Id thinks by thinking we are thinking something that is something like the thing the Id is thinking. If we can fool the Id we are all right. If not, there is no thinking what we may be thinking.

It comes to this: the things to think we think are the things that the Superego thinks are things to think and the Id thinks are things IT thinks.

I think that's perfectly clear.

• • •

Hypochondria is the only illness that I don't have.

I've always been a hypochondriac. As a little boy, I'd eat my M&Ms one by one with a glass of water.

• • •

There are three guys going through an exit interview at a psychiatric hospital. The doctor says he'll release them if they can answer the simple mathematical problem: What is 8 times 5?

The first patient says, "139".

The second one says, "Wednesday".

The third says, "What a stupid question. It's obvious: The answer is 40."

The doctor is delighted. He gives the guy his release. As the man is leaving, the doctor asks how he came up with the correct answer so quickly.

"It was easy, Doc. I just divided Wednesday into 139."

• • •

A Stanford research group advertised for participants in a study of obsessive-compulsive disorder. They were looking for therapy clients who had been diagnosed with this disorder. The response was over-whelming; they got 3 000 responses about three days after the ad came out.

All from the same person.

• • •

•••

A doctor of psychology was doing his normal rounds. He entered one of the rooms and found Patient 1 sitting on the floor, pretending to saw a piece of wood in half.

Patient 2 was hanging from the ceiling, by his feet.

The doctor asked Patient 1 what he was doing. The patient replied, "Can't you see I'm sawing this piece of wood in half?" The doctor asked Patient 1 what Patient 2 was doing. Patient 1 replied, "Oh. He's my friend, but he's a little crazy. He thinks he's a lightbulb."

The doctor looked up and, noticing Patient 2's face going all red, said, "If he's your friend, you should get him down from there before he hurts himself." To which Patient 1 replied, "What? And work in the dark?"

•••

Jake was on his deathbed. His wife, Susan, was maintaining a vigil by his side.

She held his fragile hand, and tears ran down her face.

Her praying roused him from his slumber.

He looked up and his pale lips began to move slightly.

"My darling Susan," he whispered.

"Hush, my love," she said. "Rest. Don't talk."

He was insistent. "Susan," he said in his tired voice. "I have something I must confess to you."

"There's nothing to confess," replied the weeping Susan. "Everything's all right, go to sleep."

"No, no. I must die in peace, Susan. I slept with your sister, your best friend, and your mother."

"I know," she replied. "That's why I poisoned you."

•••

As the doctor completed an examination of the patient, he said, "I can't find a cause for your complaint. Frankly, I think it's due to drinking." "In that case," said the patient, "I'll come back when you're sober."

Language and Academics

There are three kinds of people: those who can count and those who can't.

Is Hell exothermic or endothermic?

A thermodynamics professor had written a take-home exam for his graduate students. It had one question: "Is Hell exothermic (gives off heat) or endothermic (absorbs heat)? Support your answer with proof."

Most of the students wrote proofs of their beliefs using Boyle's Law (gas cools off when it expands and heats up when it is compressed) or some variant. One student, however, wrote the following:

"First, we need to know how the mass of Hell is changing in time. So, we need to know the rate that souls are moving into Hell and the rate they are leaving.

I think that we can safely assume that once a soul gets to Hell, it will not leave. Therefore, no souls are leaving. As for how many souls are entering Hell, let's look at the different religions that exist in the world today. Some of these religions state that if you are not a member of their religion, you will go to Hell. Since there are more than one of these religions and since people do not belong to more than one religion, we can project that all people and all souls will go to Hell.

With birth and death rates as they are, we can expect the number of souls in Hell to increase exponentially. Now, we look at the rate of change of the volume in Hell because Boyle's Law states that in order for the temperature and pressure in Hell to stay the same, the volume of Hell has to expand as souls are added.

This gives two possibilities:
(1) If Hell is expanding at a slower rate than the rate at which souls enter Hell, then the temperature and pressure in Hell will increase until all Hell breaks loose.
(2) Of course, if Hell is expanding at a rate faster than the increase of souls in Hell, then the temperature and pressure will drop until Hell freezes over. So which is it?

If we accept the postulate given to me by Therese Banyan during my freshman year, "that it will be a cold night in Hell before I sleep with you", and take into account the fact that I still have not succeeded in getting her into bed, then (2) cannot be true, and so Hell must be exothermic."

This student got the only A.

– *Internet Journal of Vibrational Spectroscopy*, [www.ijvs.com] 1, 5, 39 (1998)

•••

The wisdom of Steven Wright

▸ I'd kill for a Nobel Peace Prize.

▸ Borrow money from pessimists – they don't expect it back.

▸ 42.7% of all statistics are made up on the spot.

▸ A conscience is what hurts when all your other parts feel so good.

▸ All those who believe in psychokinesis, raise my hand.

▸ I almost had a psychic girlfriend but she left me before we met.

▸ OK, so what's the speed of dark?

▸ If everything seems to be going well, you've obviously overlooked something.

▸ Depression is merely anger without enthusiasm.

▸ A clear conscience is usually the sign of a bad memory.

▸ When everything is coming your way, you're in the wrong lane.

▸ Ambition is a poor excuse for not having enough sense to be lazy.

▸ Hard work pays off in the future – laziness pays off now.

▸ I intend to live forever – so far, so good.

▸ Eagles may soar, but weasels don't get sucked into jet engines.

▸ What happens if you get scared half to death twice?

▸ My mechanic told me, "I couldn't repair your brakes, so I made your horn louder."

▸ If at first you don't succeed, destroy all evidence that you tried.

▸ Experience is something you don't get until just after you need it.

▸ To steal ideas from one person is plagiarism; to steal from many is research.

▸ The sooner you fall behind, the more time you'll have to catch up.

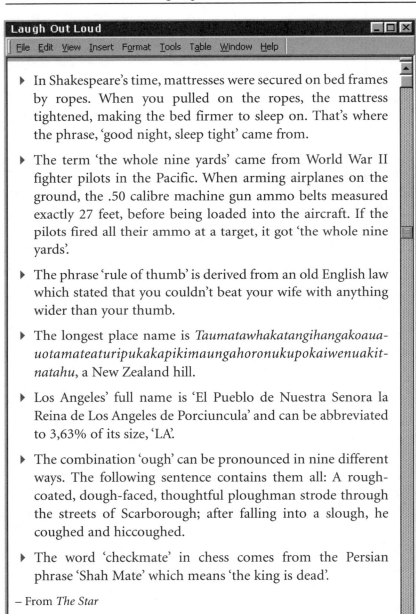

Laugh Out Loud

File Edit View Insert Format Tools Table Window Help

▶ In Shakespeare's time, mattresses were secured on bed frames by ropes. When you pulled on the ropes, the mattress tightened, making the bed firmer to sleep on. That's where the phrase, 'good night, sleep tight' came from.

▶ The term 'the whole nine yards' came from World War II fighter pilots in the Pacific. When arming airplanes on the ground, the .50 calibre machine gun ammo belts measured exactly 27 feet, before being loaded into the aircraft. If the pilots fired all their ammo at a target, it got 'the whole nine yards'.

▶ The phrase 'rule of thumb' is derived from an old English law which stated that you couldn't beat your wife with anything wider than your thumb.

▶ The longest place name is *Taumatawhakatangihangakoaua-uotamateaturipukakapikimaungahoronukupokaiwenuakit-natahu*, a New Zealand hill.

▶ Los Angeles' full name is 'El Pueblo de Nuestra Senora la Reina de Los Angeles de Porciuncula' and can be abbreviated to 3,63% of its size, 'LA'.

▶ The combination 'ough' can be pronounced in nine different ways. The following sentence contains them all: A rough-coated, dough-faced, thoughtful ploughman strode through the streets of Scarborough; after falling into a slough, he coughed and hiccoughed.

▶ The word 'checkmate' in chess comes from the Persian phrase 'Shah Mate' which means 'the king is dead'.

– From *The Star*

Some interesting facts

- Rubber bands last longer when refrigerated.
- Peanuts are one of the ingredients of dynamite.
- The national anthem of Greece has 158 verses.
- No one in Greece has memorized all 158 verses.
- There are 293 ways to make change for a dollar.
- The average secretary's left hand does 56% of the typing.
- A shark is the only fish that can blink with both eyes.
- The longest one-syllable word in the English language is 'screeched'.
- No word in the English language rhymes with: month, orange, silver or purple.
- Almonds are members of the peach family.
- Winston Churchill was born in a Ladies' Room during a dance.
- There are only four words in the English language which end in 'dous': tremendous, horrendous, stupendous, and hazardous.
- An ostrich's eye is bigger than its brain.
- Tigers have striped skin, not just striped fur.
- A dragonfly has a lifespan of 24 hours.
- A goldfish has a memory span of three seconds.
- A cat has 32 muscles in each ear.
- It's impossible to sneeze with your eyes open.
- The giant squid has the largest eyes in the world.
- In England, the Speaker of the House is not allowed to speak.
- The name for Oz in the 'Wizard of Oz' was thought up when the creator, Frank Baum, looked at his filing cabinet and saw A-N, and O-Z, hence 'Oz'.
- The microwave was invented after a researcher walked by a radar tube and a chocolate bar melted in his pocket.
- The average person falls asleep in seven minutes.
- 'Stewardesses' is the longest word that is typed with only the left hand.

•••

Is there a Santa Claus?

As a result of an overwhelming lack of requests, and with research help from that renowned scientific journal *SPY* magazine (January 1990), we are pleased to present the annual scientific enquiry into Santa Claus.

1. No known species of reindeer can fly. HOWEVER, there are 300 000 species of organisms yet to be classified, and most of these are insects and germs, so this does not COMPLETELY rule out flying reindeer which only Santa has ever seen.

2. There are about two billion children (persons under 18) in the world. BUT since Santa doesn't (appear to) handle the Muslim, Hindu, Buddhist and Jewish children, that reduces the workload to about 19% of the total – 378 million according to the Population Reference Bureau. At an average (census) rate of 3.5 children per household, that is 108 million homes. One presumes that there is at least one good child in each.

3. Santa has 31 hours of Christmas to work with, thanks to different time zones and the rotation of the earth, assuming he travels east to west (which seems logical). This works out to 968 visits per second. This is to say that, for each Christian household with good children, Santa has 1/1000th of a second to park, hop out of the sleigh, jump down the chimney, fill the stockings, distribute the remaining presents under the tree, eat whatever snacks have been left, get back up the chimney, back into the sleigh, and move on to the next house. Assuming that each of these 108 million stops are evenly distributed around the globe (which we of course know to be false but for the purposes of our calculations we will assume to be correct), we are now talking about .78 miles per household, a total trip of 84.2 million miles, not counting stops to do what most of us must do at least once every 31 hours, plus feeding, etc.

   This means that Santa's sleigh is moving at 755 miles per second, 3 700 times the speed of sound. For purposes of comparison, the fastest man-made vehicle ever produced, the Ulysses space probe, moves at a poky 27.4 miles per second, and a conventional reindeer can run, tops, 15 miles per hour.

4. The payload on the sleigh adds another interesting element. Assuming that each child gets nothing more than a medium-sized Lego set (two pounds), the sleigh is carrying 378 000 [US] tons, not counting Santa, who is invariably described as overweight. On land, conventional reindeer can pull no more than 300 pounds. Even granted that 'flying reindeer' (see point #1) can pull TEN TIMES the normal amount, we cannot do the job with eight, or even nine. We need 252 000 reindeer. This increases the payload – not even counting the weight of the sleigh – to 359 100 tons. Again, for comparison, this is four times the weight of the Queen Elizabeth.

5. 359 000 tons traveling at 755 miles per second creates enormous air resistance – this will heat the reindeer in the same fashion as spacecraft re-entering the earth's atmosphere. The lead pair of reindeer will absorb 14.3 QUINTILLION joules of energy. Per second. Each. In short, they will burst into flames almost instantaneously, exposing the reindeer behind them, and creating a deafening sonic boom in their wake. The entire reindeer team will be vaporized within 4.26 thousandths of a second. Santa, meanwhile, will be subjected to centrifugal forces 17 500.06 times greater than gravity. A 250-pound Santa (which seems ludicrously slim) would be pinned to the back of his sleigh by 4 375 015 pounds of force.

In conclusion: if Santa ever DID deliver presents on Christmas Eve, he's dead now.

•••

A cop asked me why I didn't stop at a stop sign.
I said, "I don't believe everything I read."
– Steven Wright

There are two classes of pedestrians in these days of reckless motor traffic: the quick and the dead.
– Lord Dewar

Ruin sorbees

This is a telephonic exchange between a hotel guest and room-service, at a hotel in Asia, which was recorded and published in the *Far East Economic Review*. (To be read with an Asian accent.)

ROOM SERVICE: "Morny. Ruin sorbees."

GUEST: "Sorry, I thought I dialed room-service."

ROOM SERVICE: "Rye ... Ruin sorbees ... morny! Djewish to odor sunteen??"

GUEST: "Uh ... yes ... I'd like some bacon and eggs."

ROOM SERVICE: "Ow July den?"

GUEST: "What??"

ROOM SERVICE: "Ow July den? ... pry, boy, pooch?"

GUEST: "Oh, the eggs! How do I like them? Sorry, scrambled please."

ROOM SERVICE: "Ow July dee bayhcem ... crease?"

GUEST: "Crisp will be fine."

ROOM SERVICE: "Hokay. An San tos?"

GUEST: "What?"

ROOM SERVICE: "San tos. July San tos?"

GUEST: "I don't think so."

ROOM SERVICE: "No? Judo one toes??"

GUEST: "I feel really bad about this, but I don't know what 'judo one toes' means."

ROOM SERVICE: "Toes! toes! ... why djew Don Juan toes? Ow bow singlish mopping we bother?"

GUEST: "English muffin!! I've got it! You were saying 'Toast.' Fine. Yes, an English muffin will be fine."

ROOM SERVICE: "We bother?"

GUEST: "No ... just put the bother on the side."

ROOM SERVICE: "Wad?"

GUEST: "I mean butter ... just put it on the side."

ROOM SERVICE: "Copy?"

GUEST: "Sorry?"

ROOM SERVICE:	"Copy ... tea ... mill?"
GUEST:	"Yes. Coffee please, and that's all."
ROOM SERVICE:	"One Minnie. Ass ruin torino fee, strangle ache, crease baychem, tossy singlish mopping we bother honey sigh, and copy ... rye??"
GUEST:	"Whatever you say."
ROOM SERVICE:	"Tendjewberrymud."
GUEST:	"You're welcome."

• • •

Hot cross puns

▸ Time flies like an arrow. Fruit flies like a banana.

▸ A backward poet writes inverse.

▸ She had a boyfriend with a wooden leg but broke it off.

▸ Show me a piano falling down a mineshaft and I'll show you A-flat minor.

▸ If you don't pay your exorcist, you get repossessed.

▸ The man who fell into an upholstery machine is fully recovered.

▸ You feel stuck with your debt if you can't budge it.

▸ Local Area Network in Australia: the LAN down under.

▸ The definition of a will: a dead giveaway.

▸ He often broke into song because he couldn't find the key.

▸ Every calendar's days are numbered.

▸ A plateau is a high form of flattery.

▸ The short fortune-teller who escaped from prison was a small medium at large.

▸ When you've seen one shopping center you've seen a mall.

▸ Those who jump off a Paris bridge are in Seine.

▸ Bakers trade bread recipes on a knead-to-know basis.

▸ Santa's helpers are subordinate clauses.

▸ Acupuncture is a jab well done.

▸ A bicycle can't stand alone because it is two-tired.

Do you understand why?

There is no Egg in Eggplant?
No Pine nor Apple in Pineapple
No Ham in Hamburger

English muffins weren't invented in England nor french fries in France.

Sweetmeats are sweets, while sweetbreads, which aren't sweet, are meat.

You need to be able to understand why quicksand works slowly, boxing rings are square, and a guinea pig is neither a pig nor from Guinea. And why is it that a writer writes, but fingers don't fing, grocers don't groce and hammers don't ham?

If the plural of tooth is teeth, shouldn't the plural of booth be beeth? If the teacher taught, why isn't it true that the preacher praught?

In what other language do people recite a play and play at a recital? Ship by truck and send cargo by ship; have noses that run and feet that smell?

How can a slim chance and a fat chance be the same, while a wise man and a wise guy are opposites? How can overlook and oversee be opposites while quite a lot and quite a few are alike? How can the weather be as hot as hell one day and as cold as hell the next?

And where are the people who are spring chickens or who actually would hurt a fly?

In what other language would you say your house can burn up when it actually burns down; in which you fill in a form by filling it out and in which your alarm clock goes off by going on?

Why, when we say the stars are out, they are visible, but when we say the lights are out, they are invisible?

– Samuel Murray, Cape Town

• • •

Did you know?

- In a study of 200 000 ostriches over a period of 80 years, no one reported a single case where an ostrich buried its head in the sand.
- Horses can't vomit.
- The "sixth sick sheik's sixth sheep's sick" is said to be the toughest tongue twister in the English language.
- Rats multiply so quickly that, in 18 months, two rats could have over a million descendants.
- If the government has no knowledge of aliens, then why does Title 14, Section 1211 of the Code of Federal Regulations, implemented on July 16, 1969, make it illegal for U.S. citizens to have any contact with extraterrestrials or their vehicles?
- A duck's quack doesn't echo, and no one knows why.
- Mosquito repellents don't repel. They hide you. The spray blocks the mosquito's sensors so they don't know you're there.
- The liquid inside young coconuts can be used as a substitute for blood plasma.
- No piece of paper can be folded in half more than 7 times.
- Donkeys kill more people annually than plane crashes.
- You burn more calories sleeping than you do watching television.
- It is possible to lead a cow upstairs ... but not downstairs.
- Oak trees do not produce acorns until they are fifty years of age or older.
- A Boeing 747's wingspan is longer than the Wright brothers' first flight.
- American Airlines saved $40 000 in 1987 by eliminating 1 olive from each salad served in first-class.
- Venus is the only planet that rotates clockwise.
- Apples, not caffeine, are more efficient at waking you up in the morning.
- Michael Jordan makes more money from Nike annually than all of the Nike factory workers in Malaysia combined.
- Walt Disney was afraid of mice.
- Pearls melt in vinegar.

- The reason firehouses have circular stairways is from the days when the engines were pulled by horses. The horses were stabled on the ground floor and figured out how to walk up straight staircases.
- Butterflies taste with their feet.
- In 10 minutes, a hurricane releases more energy than all of the world's nuclear weapons combined.
- Elephants are the only animals that can't jump.
- Only one person in two billion will live to be 116 or older.
- The Main Library at Indiana University sinks over an inch every year because when it was built, engineers failed to take into account the weight of all the books that would occupy the building.
- A snail can sleep for three years.
- Our eyes are always the same size from birth, but our nose and ears never stop growing.
- The electric chair was invented by a dentist.
- All polar bears are left-handed.
- 'Typewriter' is the longest word that can be made using the letters on only one row of the keyboard.
- "Go" is the shortest complete sentence in the English language.
- The cigarette lighter was invented before the match.

• • •

The manager of a large city zoo was drafting a letter to order a pair of animals. He sat at his computer and typed the following sentence: "I would like to place an order for two mongooses, to be delivered at your earliest convenience."

He stared at the screen, focusing on that odd word 'mongooses'. Then he deleted the word and added another, so the sentence now read: "I would like to place an order for two mongeese, to be delivered at your earliest convenience."

Again he stared at the screen, this time focusing on the new word, which seemed just as odd as the original one.

Finally, he deleted the whole sentence and started over again. "Everyone knows no fully stocked zoo should be without a mongoose," he typed. "Please send us two of them."

Four all who reed and right

We'll begin with a box, and the plural is boxes;
but the plural of ox became oxen not oxes.
One fowl is a goose, but two are called geese,
yet the plural of moose should never be meese.
You may find a lone mouse or a nest full of mice;
yet the plural of house is houses, not hice.

If the plural of man is always men,
why shouldn't the plural of pan be pen?
If I spoke of my foot and show you my feet,
and I give you a boot, would a pair be called beet?
If one is a tooth and a whole set are teeth,
why shouldn't the plural of booth be called beeth?

Then one may be that, and three would be those,
yet hat in the plural would never be hose,
and the plural of cat is cats, not cose.

We speak of a brother and also of brethren,
but though we say mother, we never say methren.

Then the masculine pronouns are he, his and him,
but imagine the feminine, she, shis and shim.

It had been snowing for hours when an announcement came over the intercom: "Will the students who are parked on University Drive please move their cars so that we may begin plowing." Twenty minutes later there was another announcement: "Will the nine hundred students who went to move fourteen cars please return to class."

Prejudice: A vagrant opinion without visible means of support.
– Ambrose Pierce

Jumping to conclusions

The Mathematician says, "An engineer thinks that 120 is divisible by all numbers because he sees that 120 is divisible by 1, 2, 3, 4, 5, and 6. He then checks a few more numbers taken at random, say 8, 10, 15, 20, 30 and 60. And since 120 turns out to be divisible by all these numbers he regards his experimental findings as successful and sufficient."

"Correct!" says the Engineer, "But look at the Physicist! He suspects that all odd numbers larger than 1 are prime. The first three odd numbers are 3, 5, and 7 which are prime. Then comes 9 which happens not to be a prime. But 11 and 13 are also prime. 'Let us go back to 9', says the Physicist, 'I must conclude that 9 is merely an experimental error.'"

"True," says the Physicist, "but look at the Doctor. He gave a hopelessly ill patient with uremia a bowl of mushroom soup and the patient got well. The Doctor then wrote a report on the value of mushroom soup in curing uremia. Later another uremia patient was given mushroom soup but died. In the report, the Doctor made the following correction: 'Mushroom soup helps in 50% of the cases.'"

"Yes," says the Doctor, "but the Mathematician, when asked how to catch a lion in the desert, said 'What does catching a lion mean? It means isolating the lion from yourself by means of bars. So if I get into a cage, by definition the lion is caught.'"

• • •

US government regulations, president Carter has pledged, must be written "in plain English for a change". Special workshops have been arranged for writers of regulations. James Minor, a former government lawyer, regarded as the foremost authority on "bureaucratese", is the main teacher at these workshops.

"Old regulations are almost guaranteed to be written in gobbledygook," Minor says, "because they were often drafted by lawyers who favoured sixteenth century words like 'deemed' and 'whereas' and 'aforesaid'."

This is exemplified by a paragraph that he distributes to his classes: "We respectfully petition, request and entreat that due and adequate provision be made, this day and the date hereinafter subscribed, for the satisfying of this petitioner's nutritional requirements and for the organizing of such methods as may be deemed necessary and proper to assure the reception by and for said petitioner of such quantities of baked cereal products as shall, in the judgment of the aforesaid petitioners, constitute a sufficient supply therefore."

Translated, he said, this means "Give us this day our daily bread".

— Washington Star Service

•••

Tangled tongue twister

Here is one of the world's worst – and longest – tongue-twisters. Try to read it out aloud without making a single slip.

THE SAGA OF SHREWD SIMON SHORT

Shrewd Simon Short sewed shoes. Seventeen summers, speeding storms, spreading sunshine successively, saw Simon's small, shabby shop, still standing staunch, saw Simon's selfsame squeaking sign still swinging silently specifying:

Simon Short, Smithfield's sole surviving shoemaker. Shoes sewed soled superfinely.

Simon's spry, sedulous spouse, Sally Short, sewed shirts, stitched sheets, stuffed sofas. Simon's six stout sons – Seth, Samuel, Stephen, Saul, Silas, Shadrach – sold sundries. Sober Seth sold sugar, spices; simple Sam sold saddles, stirrups, screws; sagacious Stephen sold silks, satins, shawls; skeptical Saul sold silver salvers; selfish Shadrach sold salves, shoe-strings, soap, saws, skates; slack Silas sold Sally Short's stuffed sofas.

Some seven summers since, Simon's second son Samuel saw Sophia Sophronia Spriggs somewhere. Sweet, smart, sensible Sophia

Sophronia Spriggs. Sam soon showed strong symptoms. Sam seldom stayed storing, selling saddles. Sam sighed sorrowfully, sought Sophia Sophronia's society, sung several serenades slyly. Simon stormed, scolded severely, said Sam seemed so silly singing such shameful, senseless songs. "Strange Sam should slight such splendid sales! Strutting spendthrift! Shattered-brained simpleton."

"Softly, softly, sire," said Sally. "Sam's smitten; Sam's spied some sweetheart."

"Sentimental schoolboy!" snarled Simon. "Smitten! Stop such stuff." Simon sent Sally's snuffbox spinning, seized Sally's scissors, smashed Sally's spectacles, scattering several spools. "Sneaking scoundrel! Sam's shocking silliness shall surcease!" Scowling, Simon stopped speaking, started swiftly shopward. Sally sighed sadly. Summoning Sam, she spoke sweet sympathy. "Sam," said she, "sire seems singularly snappy; so, solicit, sue, secure Sophronia speedily, Sam."

"So soon? So soon?" said Sam, standing stock-still.

"So soon, surely," said Sally smiling, "specially since sire shows such spirits."

So Sam, somewhat scared, sauntered slowly, shaking stupendously, Sam soliloquizes: "Sophia Sophronia Spriggs, Spriggs – Short – Sophia Sophronia Short – Samuel Short's spouse – sounds splendid! Suppose she should say – she shan't – she shan't!"

Soon Sam spied Sophia starching shirts, singing softly. Seeing Sam she stopped starching, saluting Sam smilingly. Sam stammered shockingly.

"Spl-spl-splendid summer season, Sophia."

"Selling saddles still, Sam?"

"Sar-sar-tin," said Sam, starting suddenly. "Season's somewhat sudorific," said Sam, steadily, staunching streaming sweat, shaking sensibly.

"Sartin," said Sophia, smiling significantly. "Sip some sweet sherbet, Sam." (Silence sixty seconds.)

"Sire shot sixty sheldrakes, Saturday," said Sophia.

"Sixty? Sho!" said Sam. (Silence seventy-seven seconds.)

"See sister Susan's sunflowers," said Sophia socially, silencing such stiff silence.

Sophia's sprightly sauciness stimulated Sam strangely: so Sam suddenly spoke sentimentally: "Sophia, Susan's sunflowers seem saying Samuel Short, Sophia Sophronia Spriggs, stroll serenely, seek some sequestered spot, some sylvan shade. Sparkling springs shall sing soul-stirring strains: sweet songsters shall silence secret sighings: super-angelic sylphs shall" – Sophia snickered; so Sam stopped.

"Sophia," said Sam solemnly.

"Sam," said Sophia.

"Sophia, stop smiling; Sam Short's sincere. Sam's seeking some sweet spouse, Sophia."

Sophia stood silent.

"Speak, Sophia, speak: such suspense speculates sorrow."

"Seek sire, Sam, seek sire."

So Sam sought sire Spriggs; sire Spriggs said, "Sartin."

– From: *A twister of twists, a tangler of tongues; tongue twisters* by Alvin Schwartz

• • •

Sign on a vending machine aboard a US Navy vessel: "If the machine is out of order, please contact the vending machine operator. Do not bang on this machine. He is not inside."

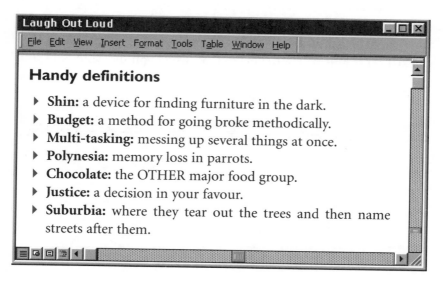

Laugh Out Loud

File Edit View Insert Format Tools Table Window Help

Handy definitions

▸ **Shin:** a device for finding furniture in the dark.
▸ **Budget:** a method for going broke methodically.
▸ **Multi-tasking:** messing up several things at once.
▸ **Polynesia:** memory loss in parrots.
▸ **Chocolate:** the OTHER major food group.
▸ **Justice:** a decision in your favour.
▸ **Suburbia:** where they tear out the trees and then name streets after them.

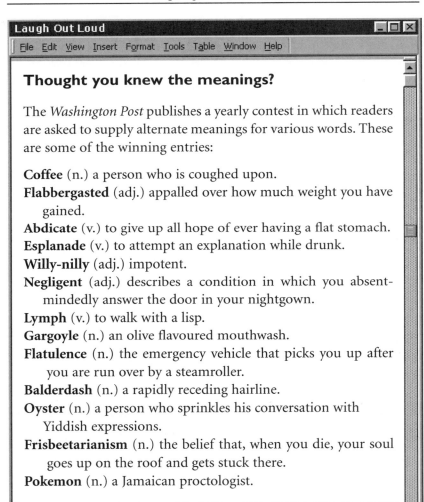

Laugh Out Loud

File Edit View Insert Format Tools Table Window Help

Thought you knew the meanings?

The *Washington Post* publishes a yearly contest in which readers are asked to supply alternate meanings for various words. These are some of the winning entries:

Coffee (n.) a person who is coughed upon.

Flabbergasted (adj.) appalled over how much weight you have gained.

Abdicate (v.) to give up all hope of ever having a flat stomach.

Esplanade (v.) to attempt an explanation while drunk.

Willy-nilly (adj.) impotent.

Negligent (adj.) describes a condition in which you absent-mindedly answer the door in your nightgown.

Lymph (v.) to walk with a lisp.

Gargoyle (n.) an olive flavoured mouthwash.

Flatulence (n.) the emergency vehicle that picks you up after you are run over by a steamroller.

Balderdash (n.) a rapidly receding hairline.

Oyster (n.) a person who sprinkles his conversation with Yiddish expressions.

Frisbeetarianism (n.) the belief that, when you die, your soul goes up on the roof and gets stuck there.

Pokemon (n.) a Jamaican proctologist.

Talk is cheap *because supply exceeds demand.*

If you can't *be kind, at least have the decency to be vague.*

Don't believe the bulletins

These are actual announcements taken from church bulletins:

1. Would the congregation please note that the bowl at the back of the church labelled "For The Sick" is for monetary donations only.
2. Don't let worry kill you. Let the church help.
3. Thursday night potluck supper. Prayer and medication to follow.
4. For those of you who have children and don't know it, we have a nursery downstairs.
5. This afternoon there will be a meeting in the south and north ends of the church. Children will be baptized at both ends.
6. Thursday at 5 pm there will be a meeting of the Little Mothers Club. All wishing to become Little Mothers, please see the minister in his private study.
7. Tuesday at 4 pm there will be an ice cream social. All ladies giving milk please come early.
8. This being Easter Sunday, we will ask Mrs Lewis to come forward and lay an egg on the altar.
9. Next Sunday, a special collection will be taken to defray the cost of the new carpet. All those wishing to do something on the new carpet will come forward and get a piece of paper.
10. The ladies of the church have cast off clothing of every kind and they may be seen in the church basement Friday.
11. At the evening service tonight, the sermon topic will be: 'What Is Hell?' Come early and listen to our choir practise.
12. Weight Watchers will meet at 7 pm at the First Presbyterian Church. Please use the large double door at the side entrance.
13. Pastor is on vacation. Massages can be given to the church secretary.
14. Scouts are saving aluminum cans, bottles, and other items to be recycled. Proceeds will be used to cripple children.
15. The Associate Minister unveiled the church's new tithing campaign slogan last Sunday: "I Upped My Pledge – Up Yours!"

• • •

Maths through the decades

Teaching Maths in 1950:
A logger sells a truckload of lumber for $100. His cost of production is ⅘ of the price. What is his profit?

Teaching Maths in 1960:
A logger sells a truckload of lumber for $100. His cost of production is ⅘ of the price, or $80. What is his profit?

Teaching Maths in 1970:
A logger exchanges a set "L" of lumber for a set "M" of money. The cardinality of set "M" is 100. Each element is worth one dollar. Make 100 dots representing the elements of the set "M". The set "C", the cost of production, contains 20 fewer points than set "M". Represent the set "C" as a subset of set "M" and answer the following question: What is the cardinality of the set "P" for profits?

Teaching Maths in 1980:
A logger sells a truckload of lumber for $100. Her cost of production is $80 and her profit is $20. Your assignment: Underline the number 20.

Teaching Maths in 1990:
By cutting down beautiful forest trees, the logger makes $20. What do you think of this way of making a living? Topic for class participation after answering the question: How did the forest birds and squirrels feel as the logger cut down the trees? There are no wrong answers.

Teaching Maths in 1996:
By laying off 40% of its loggers, a company improves its stock price from $80 to $100. How much capital gain per share does the CEO make by exercising his stock options at $80? Assume capital gains are no longer taxed, because this encourages investment.

Teaching Maths in 1997:
A company outsources all of its loggers. The firm saves on benefits, and when demand for its product is down, the logging workforce can easily be cut back. The average logger employed by the company

earned \$50 000, had three weeks vacation, a nice retirement plan and medical insurance. The contracted logger charges \$50 an hour. Was outsourcing a good move?

Teaching Maths in 1998:
A laid-off logger with four kids at home and a ridiculous alimony from his first failed marriage comes into the logging company's corporate office and goes postal, mowing down 16 executives and a couple of secretaries, and gets lucky when he nails a politician on the premises collecting his kickback. Was outsourcing the loggers a good move for the company?

Teaching Maths in 1999:
A laid-off logger serving time in prison for blowing away several people is being trained as a COBOL programmer in order to work on Y2K projects. What is the probability that the automatic cell doors will open on their own as of 00:01, 01/01/00?

• • •

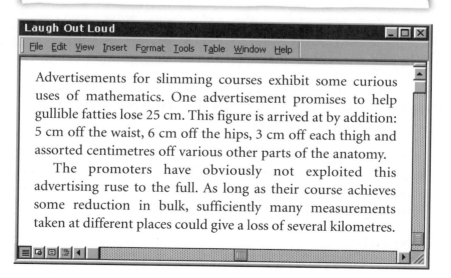

2 + 2 = 5 for very large values of 2.

Laugh Out Loud

File   Edit   View   Insert   Format   Tools   Table   Window   Help

Advertisements for slimming courses exhibit some curious uses of mathematics. One advertisement promises to help gullible fatties lose 25 cm. This figure is arrived at by addition: 5 cm off the waist, 6 cm off the hips, 3 cm off each thigh and assorted centimetres off various other parts of the anatomy.

The promoters have obviously not exploited this advertising ruse to the full. As long as their course achieves some reduction in bulk, sufficiently many measurements taken at different places could give a loss of several kilometres.

Bad newspaper headlines

▶ March Planned For Next August
▶ Patient At Death's Door – Doctors Pull Him Through
▶ Juvenile Court to Try Shooting Defendant
▶ 20-Year Friendship Ends at Altar
▶ Blind Woman Gets New Kidney from Dad She Hasn't Seen in Years
▶ Defendant's Speech Ends in Long Sentence
▶ Police Begin Campaign to Run Down Jaywalkers
▶ Police Discover Crack in Australia
▶ William Kelly, 87, was Fed Secretary
▶ Collegians are Turning to Vegetables
▶ Quarter of a Million Chinese Live on Water
▶ Caribbean Islands Drift to Left
▶ Red Tape Holds Up New Bridge
▶ Typhoon Rips Through Cemetery; Hundreds Dead
▶ Kids Make Nutritious Snacks
▶ Local High School Dropouts Cut In Half

• • •

Why did the chicken cross the road?

SAEED AL SAHAF (Iraqi Head of Information)
The chicken did not cross the road. This is a complete fabrication. In fact, we do not even have a chicken.

GEORGE W. BUSH
We don't care why the chicken crossed the road. We just want to know if the chicken is on our side of the road or not. The chicken is either for us or against us. There is no middle ground.

TONY BLAIR
I agree with George.

JOHN HOWARD
I agree with George and Tony.

COLIN POWELL (United States Secretary of State)
Now to the left of the screen, you can clearly see the satellite image of the chicken crossing the road.

FORMER VICE-PRESIDENT GORE
I fight for chickens and, even though I have lost the race for the White House, I will continue fighting for chickens. I will fight for chickens and I will not disappoint them.

SADDAM HUSSEIN
This was an unprovoked act of rebellion, and we were quite justified in dropping 50 tons of nerve gas on it.

MARTIN LUTHER KING, JR
I envision a world where all chickens will be free to cross without having their motives called into question.

CAPTAIN JAMES T. KIRK
To boldly go where no chicken has gone before.

FOX MULDER
You saw it cross the road with your own eyes. How many more chickens have to cross before you believe it?

GRANDPA
In my day, we didn't ask why the chicken crossed the road. Somebody told us the chicken crossed the road, and that was good enough.

ERNEST HEMINGWAY
To die. In the rain.

JOHN LENNON
Imagine all the chickens, crossing all the roads. You may say I'm a dreamer – but it's not the only hen.

KARL MARX
It was an historic inevitability.

ARISTOTLE
It is the nature of chickens to cross the road.

DR SEUSS
Did the chicken cross the road?
Did he cross it with a toad?
Yes! The chicken crossed the road,
But why it crossed, I've not been told!

SIGMUND FREUD
The fact that you are at all concerned that the chicken crossed the road reveals your underlying sexual insecurity.

OPRAH
Isn't that interesting? In a few moments, we will be listening to the chicken tell, for the first time, the heart-warming story of how it felt accomplishing its lifelong dream of crossing the road.

RONALD REAGAN
What chicken?

BILL GATES
eChicken200X version 1.0 will not only cross roads, but will lay eggs, file your important documents, and balance your cheque book – and Internet Explorer is an integral part of eChicken.

ALEX FERGUSON
The chicken was not drawn to the other side fairly, and Beckham is not bigger than this club.

THE BIBLE
And God came down from heaven, and he said unto the chicken THOU SHALT CROSS THE ROAD. And the chicken didst cross the road, and there was much rejoicing.

ALBERT EINSTEIN
Did the chicken really cross the road, or did the road move beneath the chicken?

BILL CLINTON
I did not cross the road with THAT chicken. What do you mean by "chicken"? Could you define "chicken"?

COLONEL SANDERS
Did I miss one?

HOMER SIMPSON
Mmmmmmmmm ... c h i c k e n

• • •

Catch-22

One day, a group of eminent scientists got together and decided that Man had come a long way and no longer needed God. So they picked one of their number to go and tell Him that they were done with Him.

The scientist walked up to God and said, "God, we've decided that we have advanced to the point that we no longer need you. We can clone people and do many miraculous things, so why don't you just retire?"

God listened very patiently, and then said, "Very well, I will agree if you can demonstrate your proficiency to me. Let's have a man-making contest."

The scientist replied, "Sounds good!" God added, "Now, we're going to do this just like I did back in the old days with Adam."

"Of course," said the scientist, and bent down and grabbed himself a handful of dirt.

God just looked at him and said, "No, no, no ... You get your OWN dirt!"

The following are actual excerpts from classified sections of various city newspapers.

Auto Repair Service. Free pick-up and delivery. Try us once, you'll never go anywhere again.

Dog for sale: eats anything and is fond of children.

Man wanted to work in dynamite factory. Must be willing to travel.

Girl wanted to assist magician in cutting-off-head illusion. Blue Cross and salary.

We do not tear your clothing with machinery. We do it carefully by hand.

Tired of cleaning yourself? Let me do it.

Used Cars: Why go elsewhere to be cheated. Come here first.

Wanted. Man to take care of cow that does not smoke or drink.

We will oil your sewing machine and adjust tension in your home for $5.00.

VACATION SPECIAL: have your home exterminated.

• • •

I started out with nothing and still have most of it left.

Final examination

Instructions: Read each question carefully. Answer all questions. Time limit: 2 hours. Begin immediately.

History – Describe the history of the Papacy from its origins to the present day, concentrating especially, but not exclusively, on its social, political, economic, religious and philosophical impact on Europe, Asia, America and Africa. Be brief, concise and specific.

Biology – Create life. Estimate the differences in subsequent human culture if this form of life had developed 500 million years earlier, with special attention to its probable effect on the English Parliamentary System. Prove your thesis.

Music – Write a piano concerto. Orchestrate and perform it with flute and drum. You will find a piano under your seat.

Sociology – Estimate the sociological problems which might accompany the end of the world. Construct an experiment to test your theory.

Civil Engineering – This is a practical test of your design and building skills. With the boxes of toothpicks and glue present, build a platform that will support your weight when you and your platform are suspended over a vat of nitric acid.

Economics – Develop a realistic plan for refinancing the national debt. Trace the possible effects of your plan in the following areas: Cubism, the Donatist Controversy and the Wave Theory of Light. Outline a method for preventing these effects. Criticize this method from all possible points of view. Point out the deficiencies in your point of view, as demonstrated in your answer to the last question.

Political Science – There is a red telephone on the desk beside you. Start World War III. Report at length on its socio-political effects, if any.

Philosophy – Sketch the development of human thought. Estimate its significance. Compare with the development of any other kind of thought.

Epistemology – Take a position for or against truth. Prove the validity of your stand.

Religion – Perform a miracle. Creativity will be judged.

Metaphysics – Describe in detail the probable nature of life after death. Test your hypothesis.

Art – Given one eight-count box of crayons and three sheets of notebook paper, recreate the ceiling of the Sistine Chapel. Skin tones should be true to life.

General Knowledge – Describe in detail. Be objective and specific.

Extra Credit – Define the universe, and give three examples.

• • •

First one out!

All the greatest scientists who ever lived are in heaven and decide to play hide-'n-seek.

To start off, Einstein is the one who has the den. He is supposed to count up to 100 and then start searching.

Everyone starts hiding except Newton, who just draws a square of 1 metre and stands in it right in front of Einstein.

Einstein counts ... 97, 98, 99, 100.

He opens his eyes and finds Newton standing in front of him.

Einstein says, "Newton's out! Newton's out!"

Newton denies this and states categorically he is not out, on the basis that he is not Newton.

All the scientists come out and he goes on to prove that he is not Newton ... How does he do it?

Newton says:

I am standing in a square of area 1 metre square.

That means there is 1 Newton per metre square ...

Since 1 Newton per metre square = 1 Pascal, I am Pascal; hence PASCAL is out.

A grandchild's guide to using Grandpa's computer

Bits Bytes Chips Clocks
Bits in bytes on chips in box.
Bytes with bits and chips with clocks.
Chips in box on ether-docks.

Chips with bits come. Chips with bytes come.
Chips with bits and bytes and clocks come.

Look, sir. Look, sir. Read the book, sir.
Let's do tricks with bits and bytes, sir.
Let's do tricks with chips and clocks, sir.

First, I'll make a quick trick bit stack.
Then I'll make a quick trick byte stack.
You can make a quick trick chip stack.
You can make a quick trick clock stack.

And here's a new trick on the scene.
Bits in bytes for your machine.
Bytes in words to fill your screen.

Now we come to ticks and tocks, sir.
Try to say this by the clock, sir.

Clocks on chips tick.
Clocks on chips tock.
Eight byte bits tick.
Eight bit bytes tock.
Clocks on chips with eight bit bytes tick.
Chips with clocks and eight byte bits tock.

Here's an easy game to play.
Here's an easy thing to say ...

If a packet hits a pocket on a socket on a port,
and the bus is interrupted as a very last resort,
and the address of the memory
makes your floppy disk abort
then the socket packet pocket
has an error to report!

If your cursor finds a menu item
followed by a dash,
and the double-clicking icon
puts your window in the trash,
and your data is corrupted cause
the index doesn't hash,
then your situation's hopeless,
and your system's gunna crash.

You can't say this? What a shame, sir!
We'll find you another game, sir.

If the label on the cable
on the table at your house
says the network is connected
to the button on your mouse,
but your packets want to tunnel
on another protocol,
that's repeatedly rejected
by the printer down the hall,
and your screen is all distorted
by the side-effects of gauss,
so your icons in the window
are as wavy as a souse,
then you may as well reboot
and go out with a bang,
cause as sure as I'm a poet,
the sucker's gunna hang!

When the copy of your floppy's
getting sloppy on the disk,
and the microcode instructions
cause unnecessary risc,
then you have to flash your memory
and you'll want to RAM your ROM.
quickly turn off your computer
and be sure to tell your mom!

– Gene Ziegler
(http://www.people.cornell.edu/pages/elz1/clocktower/)

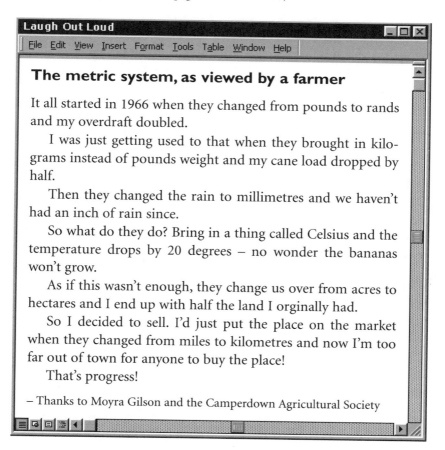

Laugh Out Loud

File Edit View Insert Format Tools Table Window Help

The metric system, as viewed by a farmer

It all started in 1966 when they changed from pounds to rands and my overdraft doubled.

I was just getting used to that when they brought in kilo-grams instead of pounds weight and my cane load dropped by half.

Then they changed the rain to millimetres and we haven't had an inch of rain since.

So what do they do? Bring in a thing called Celsius and the temperature drops by 20 degrees – no wonder the bananas won't grow.

As if this wasn't enough, they change us over from acres to hectares and I end up with half the land I orginally had.

So I decided to sell. I'd just put the place on the market when they changed from miles to kilometres and now I'm too far out of town for anyone to buy the place!

That's progress!

– Thanks to Moyra Gilson and the Camperdown Agricultural Society

When someone says "have a nice day", tell them
you have other plans.

New scientific developments

These are supposedly responses to a contest sponsored by *OMNI* magazine. Strangely, these scientific developments were never considered by the Nobel Committee.

GRAND PRIZE WINNER

Antigravity
When a cat is dropped, it always lands on its feet, and when toast is dropped, it always lands with the buttered side facing down. It is proposed to strap buttered toast to the back of a cat; the two will hover, spinning inches above the ground. With a giant buttered cat array, a high-speed monorail could easily link New York with Chicago.

RUNNERS-UP

Rednecks and Braille
If an infinite number of rednecks riding in an infinite number of pickup trucks fire an infinite number of shotgun rounds at an infinite number of highway signs, they will eventually produce all the world's great literary works in Braille.

Why yawning is contagious
You yawn to equalize the pressure on your eardrums. This pressure change outside your eardrums unbalances other people's ear pressures, so they must yawn to even it out.

• • •

Nostalgia isn't what it used to be.

Life,
Wisdom and
Motivation

Always remember you're unique ... just like everyone else.

A lesson in time management

A speaker stood in front of a group of high-powered over-achievers and said, "Okay, time for a quiz".

He pulled out a one-gallon, wide-mouthed mason jar and set it on a table in front of him. He produced about a dozen fist-sized rocks and carefully placed them, one at a time, into the jar.

When the jar was filled to the top and no more rocks could fit inside, he asked, "Is this jar full?"

Everyone in the class said, "Yes."

Then he said, "Really?"

He reached under the table and pulled out a bucket of gravel. He dumped some gravel in and shook the jar causing pieces of gravel to work themselves down into the spaces between the big rocks.

He smiled and asked the group once more, "Is the jar full?"

By this time, the class was onto him. "Probably not," one of them answered.

"Good!" he replied. He reached under the table and brought out a bucket of sand. He dumped the sand in and it went into all the spaces left between the rocks and the gravel.

Once more he asked the question, "Is this jar full?"

"No!" the class shouted.

Once again he said, "Good!"

Then he grabbed a pitcher of water and began to pour it in until the jar was filled to the brim.

He looked up at the class and asked, "What is the point of this illustration?"

One eager beaver raised his hand and said, "The point is, no matter how full your schedule is, if you try really hard, you can always fit some more things into it!"

"No," the speaker replied, "that's not the point. What this illustration teaches us is that if you don't put the big rocks in first, you'll never get them in at all."

• • •

To understand is to forgive – even oneself.
– Alexander Chase

*A difference of tastes in jokes is a great strain
on the affections.*
– George Eliot

*Don't be afraid to take a big step if one is indicated.
You can't cross a chasm in two small jumps.*
– Ashley Brilliant

Talk to a man about himself and he will listen for hours.
– Benjamin Disraeli

*Friendship will not stand the strain of very much
good advice for very long.*
– Robert Lynd

*No man really knows about other human beings.
The best he can do is suppose that they are like himself.*
– John Steinbeck

*Sometimes the most urgent and vital thing you
can possibly do is take a complete rest.*
– Ashley Brilliant

*Even if you're on the right track, you'll get run over
if you just sit there.*
– Will Rogers

This is the tomorrow you worried about yesterday.
– Ashley Brilliant

Live out of your imagination, not your history.
– Stephen Covey

Three great lessons

ONE

During my second month of nursing school, our professor gave us a pop quiz. I was a conscientious student and had breezed through the questions, until I read the last one: "What is the first name of the woman who cleans the school?"

Surely this was some kind of joke. I had seen the cleaning woman several times. She was tall, dark-haired and in her 50s, but how would I know her name? I handed in my paper, leaving the last question blank.

Just before class ended, one student asked if the last question would count towards our quiz grade. "Absolutely," said the professor. "In your careers, you will meet many people. All are significant. They deserve your attention and care, even if all you do is smile and say 'Hello.'" I've never forgotten that lesson. I also learned her name was Dorothy.

TWO

One night, at 11:30 pm, an older African American woman was standing on the side of an Alabama highway trying to endure a lashing rain storm. Her car had broken down and she desperately needed a ride. Soaking wet, she decided to flag down the next car. A young white man stopped to help her, generally unheard of in those conflict-filled 1960s. The man took her to safety, helped her get assistance and put her into a taxi cab. She seemed to be in a big hurry, but wrote down his address and thanked him.

Seven days went by and a knock came on the man's door. To his surprise, a giant console colour TV was delivered to his home. A special note was attached. It read: "Thank you so much for assisting me on the highway the other night. The rain drenched not only my clothes, but also my spirits. Then you came along. Because of you, I was able to make it to my dying husband's bedside just before he passed away. God bless you for helping me and unselfishly serving others."

Sincerely,
Mrs. Nat King Cole

THREE

Many years ago, when I worked as a volunteer at a hospital, I got to know a little girl named Liz who was suffering from a rare and serious disease.

Her only chance of recovery appeared to be a blood transfusion from her 5-year-old brother, who had miraculously survived the same disease and had developed the antibodies needed to combat the illness. The doctor explained the situation to her little brother and asked the little boy if he would be willing to give his blood to his sister.

I saw him hesitate for only a moment before taking a deep breath and saying, "Yes, I'll do it if it will save her." As the transfusion progressed, he lay in bed next to his sister and smiled, as we all did, seeing the colour returning to her cheeks. Then his face grew pale and his smile faded. He looked up at the doctor and asked with a trembling voice, "Will I start to die right away?" Being young, the little boy had misunderstood the doctor; he thought he was going to have to give his sister all of his blood in order to save her.

• • •

Daily prayer

Dear God,

So far today, I've done all right. I haven't gossiped, I haven't lost my temper, I haven't been greedy, grumpy, nasty, or self-centred. I'm really happy about that so far.

But, in a few minutes Lord, I'm going to be getting out of bed. And then I am going to need a lot of help.

Thank You,
Amen

The only difference between a rut and a grave is the depth.

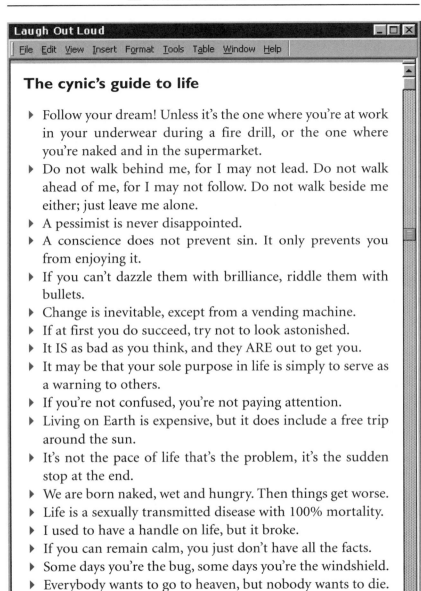

Laugh Out Loud

File Edit View Insert Format Tools Table Window Help

The cynic's guide to life

▶ Follow your dream! Unless it's the one where you're at work in your underwear during a fire drill, or the one where you're naked and in the supermarket.

▶ Do not walk behind me, for I may not lead. Do not walk ahead of me, for I may not follow. Do not walk beside me either; just leave me alone.

▶ A pessimist is never disappointed.

▶ A conscience does not prevent sin. It only prevents you from enjoying it.

▶ If you can't dazzle them with brilliance, riddle them with bullets.

▶ Change is inevitable, except from a vending machine.

▶ If at first you do succeed, try not to look astonished.

▶ It IS as bad as you think, and they ARE out to get you.

▶ It may be that your sole purpose in life is simply to serve as a warning to others.

▶ If you're not confused, you're not paying attention.

▶ Living on Earth is expensive, but it does include a free trip around the sun.

▶ It's not the pace of life that's the problem, it's the sudden stop at the end.

▶ We are born naked, wet and hungry. Then things get worse.

▶ Life is a sexually transmitted disease with 100% mortality.

▶ I used to have a handle on life, but it broke.

▶ If you can remain calm, you just don't have all the facts.

▶ Some days you're the bug, some days you're the windshield.

▶ Everybody wants to go to heaven, but nobody wants to die.

The rules for being human

When you were born, you didn't come with an owner's manual; these guidelines make life work better.

1. You will receive a body. You may like it or hate it, but it's the only thing you are sure to keep for the rest of your life.
2. You will learn lessons. You are enrolled in a full-time informal school called 'Life on Planet Earth'. Every person or incident is the Universal Teacher.
3. There are no mistakes, only lessons. Growth is a process of experimentation. 'Failures' are as much a part of the process as 'Success'.
4. A lesson is repeated until learned. It is presented to you in various forms until you learn it – then you can go on to the next lesson.
5. If you don't learn easy lessons, they get harder. External problems are a precise reflection of your internal state. When you clear inner obstructions, your outside world changes. Pain is how the universe gets your attention.
6. You will know you have learned a lesson when your actions change. Wisdom is practice. A little of something is better than nothing.
7. 'There' is no better than 'Here'. When your 'There' becomes a 'Here', you will simply obtain another 'There' that looks better than 'Here'.
8. Others are only a mirror of you. You cannot love or hate something about another, unless it reflects something you love or hate in yourself.
9. Your life is up to you. Life provides the canvas; you do the painting. Take charge of your life – or someone else will.
10. You always get what you want. Your subconscious rightfully determines what energies, experiences, and people you attract; therefore the only foolproof way to know what you want is to see what you have. There are no victims – only students.

11. There is no right or wrong, but there are consequences. Moralising doesn't help; judgements only hold the patterns in place. Just do your best.

12. Your answers lie inside you. Children need guidance from others; as we mature we must trust our hearts, where the Laws of the Spirit are written. You know more than you have heard or read or been told. All you need to do is look, listen and trust.

13. You may forget all of this.

14. You can remember anytime you wish.

– Based on *The Rules of Life* by Dr Cherie Carter-Scott

• • •

The pond

An old farmer had owned a large farm for several years. He had a pond at the back, done up nicely; picnic tables, horseshoe courts, basketball court, and so on. The pond was properly shaped and fixed up for swimming when it was built.

One evening the old farmer decided to go down to the pond to look it over, as he hadn't been there for a while.

As he neared the pond, he heard voices shouting and laughing with glee. As he came closer he saw a bunch of young women skinny dipping. He made the women aware of his presence and they all went to the deep end of the pond.

One of the women shouted to him, "We're not coming out until you leave!"

The old man replied, "I didn't come down here to watch you ladies swim or make you get out of the pond naked.

I only came to feed the alligator."

Moral: Old age and treachery will triumph over youth and inexperience.

• • •

Some wise words

1. Don't worry about what people think, they don't do it very often.
2. Artificial intelligence is no match for natural stupidity.
3. My idea of housework is to sweep the room with a glance.
4. If you look like your passport picture, you probably need the trip.
5. Bills travel through the mail at twice the speed of cheques.
6. Men are from earth. Women are from earth. Deal with it.
7. No man has ever been shot while doing the dishes.
8. A balanced diet is a cookie in each hand.
9. Middle age is when broadness of the mind and narrowness of the waist change places.
10. Opportunities always look bigger going than coming.
11. Junk is something you've kept for years and throw away three weeks before you need it.
12. There is always one more idiot than you counted on.
13. Experience is the ability to recognize a mistake when you make it again.
14. Someone who thinks logically provides a nice contrast to the real world.
15. By the time you can make ends meet, they move the ends.
16. If you must choose between two evils, pick the one you've never tried before.
17. Smile, it's the second best thing you can do with your lips.
18. Good judgement comes from bad experience, and a lot of that comes from bad judgement.
19. If you tell the truth, you don't have to remember anything.
20. Duct tape is like the Force. It has a light side and a dark side, and it holds the universe together.
21. Never miss a good chance to shut up.
22. If at first you don't succeed, give up. No sense in being a fool about it.

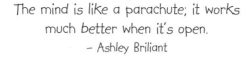

The mind is like a parachute; it works
much better when it's open.
– Ashley Briliant

'Tis better to be thought a fool, than to open your mouth
and remove all doubt.

What I've learned as I've matured

▸ You cannot make someone love you. All you can do is stalk them and hope they panic and give in.

▸ No matter how much I care, some people are just idiots.

▸ It takes years to build up trust, and it takes only suspicion, not proof, to destroy it.

▸ You shouldn't compare yourself to others – they are more screwed up than you think.

▸ We are responsible for what we do, unless we are celebrities.

▸ Regardless of how hot and steamy a relationship is at first, the passion fades, and there had better be a lot of money to take its place.

▸ The people you care most about in life are taken from you too soon and all the less important ones just never go away.

▸ A closed mouth gathers no feet.

▸ The young know the rules, the old know the exceptions.

▸ It's hard to make a comeback when you haven't been anywhere.

▸ If there's a will, I want to be in it.

▸ It's lonely at the top, but you eat better.

▸ You can keep vomiting long after you think you're finished.

▸ Consciousness is that annoying time between naps.

▸ It's all fun and games, until someone loses an eye! Then it's a 'sport'!

▸ Life is an endless struggle full of frustrations and challenges, but eventually you find a hairstylist you like.

- If at first you don't succeed, see if the loser gets anything.
- You don't stop laughing because you grow old; you grow old because you stop laughing.
- I don't mind the rat race, but I could do with a little more cheese.
- Blessed are those who hunger and thirst, for they are sticking to their diets.
- It is far more impressive when others discover your good qualities without your help.
- Age doesn't always bring wisdom. Sometimes age comes alone.
- Life not only begins at forty, it begins to show.
- Before you criticize someone, you should walk a mile in their shoes. That way, when you criticize them, you're a mile away and you have their shoes.
- Age is important only if you're cheese or wine.
- It is much easier to apologize than to ask permission.
- There are two rules for ultimate success in life. Never tell everything you know.
- I can please only one person per day. Today is not your day. Tomorrow isn't looking good either.

• • •

Rudeness is a weak imitation of strength.
– Eric Hoffer

No trumpets sound when the important decisions of our life are made. Destiny is made known silently.
– Agnes DeMille

One of the symptoms of an approaching nervous breakdown is the belief that one's work is terribly important.
– Bertrand Russell

The farmer's donkey

One day a farmer's donkey fell down into a well. The animal cried piteously for hours as the farmer tried to figure out what to do.

Finally he decided the animal was old, and the well needed to be covered up anyway; it just wasn't worth it to retrieve the donkey. He invited all his neighbours to come over and help him. They all grabbed a shovel and began to shovel dirt into the well. At first, the donkey realized what was happening and cried horribly. Then, to everyone's amazement, he quietened down.

A few shovel loads later, the farmer finally looked down into the well, and was astonished at what he saw. With every shovel of dirt that hit his back, the donkey was doing something amazing. He would shake it off and take a step up. As the farmer's neighbours continued to shovel dirt on top of the animal, he would shake it off and take a step up. Pretty soon, everyone was amazed as the donkey stepped up over the edge of the well and trotted off!

Moral: What happens to you isn't nearly as important as how you react to it. Life is going to shovel all kinds of dirt on you – but you can get out of the deepest wells by never giving up!

P.S.: The donkey later came back and kicked the hell out of the farmer who tried burying him.

Moral: When you try to cover your ass, it'll come back to get you ...

• • •

So I was getting into my car, and this bloke says to me "Can you give me a lift?" I said "Sure. You look great. The world's your oyster. Go for it."

Watch your thoughts, they *become* words.
Watch your words, they *become* actions.
Watch your actions, they *become* habits.
Watch your habits, they *become* character.

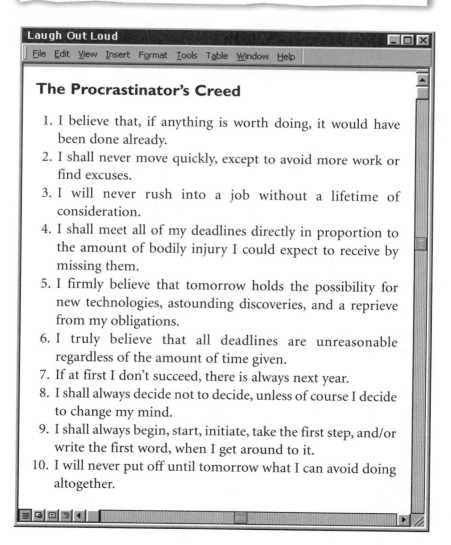

Laugh Out Loud

File   Edit   View   Insert   Format   Tools   Table   Window   Help

The Procrastinator's Creed

1. I believe that, if anything is worth doing, it would have been done already.
2. I shall never move quickly, except to avoid more work or find excuses.
3. I will never rush into a job without a lifetime of consideration.
4. I shall meet all of my deadlines directly in proportion to the amount of bodily injury I could expect to receive by missing them.
5. I firmly believe that tomorrow holds the possibility for new technologies, astounding discoveries, and a reprieve from my obligations.
6. I truly believe that all deadlines are unreasonable regardless of the amount of time given.
7. If at first I don't succeed, there is always next year.
8. I shall always decide not to decide, unless of course I decide to change my mind.
9. I shall always begin, start, initiate, take the first step, and/or write the first word, when I get around to it.
10. I will never put off until tomorrow what I can avoid doing altogether.

> Each generation imagines itself to be more intelligent than the one that went before it, and wiser than the one that comes after it.
> – George Orwell

> Man arrives as a novice at each age of his life.
> – Chamfort

• • •

11 rules of life

1. Never give yourself a haircut after three margaritas.
2. You need only two tools: Q20 and duct tape. If it doesn't move and it should, use Q20. If it moves and shouldn't, use duct tape.
3. The five most essential words for a healthy, vital relationship are "I apologize" and "You are right".
4. Everyone seems normal until you get to know them.
5. Never pass up an opportunity to go to the toilet.
6. If he/she says that you are too good for him/her – believe them.
7. Learn to pick your battles. Ask yourself: "Will this matter one year from now? How about one month? One week? One day?"
8. When you make a mistake, make amends immediately. It's easier to eat crow while it's still warm.
9. If you woke up breathing, congratulations! You have another chance!
10. Living well really is the best revenge. Being miserable because of a bad or former relationship just might mean that the other person was right about you.
11. And finally ... be really good to your family and/or friends. You never know when you are going to need them to empty your bedpan.

• • •

Pearls of wisdom

▸ In theory, theory and practice are the same. In practice, they're not.

▸ If the human brain were simple enough for us to understand, we would still be so stupid that we wouldn't understand it.

▸ There is absolutely no substitute for a genuine lack of preparation.

▸ The amount of sleep required by the average person is about five minutes more.

▸ A racehorse is an animal that can take several thousand people for a ride at the same time.

▸ A good way to get your name in the newspaper is to cross the street reading one.

▸ The trouble with getting to work on time is that it makes the day so long.

▸ To really know a man, observe his behaviour with a woman, a flat tyre, and a child.

▸ Human beings, who are almost unique in their ability to learn from the experience of others, are also remarkable for their apparent disinclination to do so.

▸ No matter what you do, someone always knew you would.

▸ Judge each day, not by the harvest, but by the seeds you plant.

▸ Don't talk unless you can improve the silence.

▸ Many a man creates his own lack of opportunity.

▸ If you don't enjoy what you have, how could you be happier with more?

• • •

It is not an optical illusion, it just looks like one.
 – Phil White

Truth is. Belief is not required.
 – Gerry Roston

25 ways to reduce stress

1. Go to bed on time.
2. Get up on time so you can start the day unrushed.
3. Say "no" to projects that won't fit into your time schedule, or that will compromise your mental and emotional health.
4. Delegate tasks to capable others.
5. Simplify and unclutter your life.
6. Allow extra time to do things and to get to places.
7. Pace yourself. Spread out big changes and difficult projects over time; don't lump the hard things all together.
8. Slow down and take one day at a time.
9. Live within your budget.
10. Have backups; an extra car key in your wallet, an extra house key buried in the garden, extra stamps, etc.
11. K.M.S. (Keep Mouth Shut). This single piece of advice can prevent an enormous amount of trouble.
12. Do something for the kid in you everyday.
13. Get enough exercise and eat right.
14. Get organized so everything has its place.
15. Listen to a tape while driving that can help improve your quality of life.
16. Find time to be alone.
17. Make friends with positive people.
18. Laugh.
19. Laugh some more!
20. Take your work seriously, but yourself not at all.
21. Develop a forgiving attitude (most people are doing the best they can).
22. Sit on your ego.
23. Talk less; listen more.
24. Remind yourself that you are not the general manager of the universe.
25. Every night before bed, think of one thing you're grateful for that you've never been grateful for before.

Everything
Else

Lead me not into temptation – I can find it myself.

The wandering monk

A wandering monk walked barefoot everywhere he went, to the point that the soles of his feet eventually became quite thick and leathery. And because he ate very little, he gradually became very frail. Several days often passed between opportunities to brush his teeth, so he usually had bad breath. Therefore, throughout the region, he came to be known as the super-calloused fragile mystic plagued with halitosis.

• • •

Five Germans travelling through Italy in an Audi Quattro are stopped at a roadblock: "It'sa illegala to putta 5 people in a Quattro."

"Vot do you mean it'z illegal?" asks the German driver.

"Quattro meansa four," replies the Italian traffic officer.

"Qvattro is just ze name of ze automobile," the Germans retort unbelievingly. "Look at ze papers: zis car is designt to kerry 5 persons."

"You can'ta pulla thata one on me!" says the officer. "Quattro meansa four. You hava fiva people ina your car and you are therefora breaking the law."

The German driver replies angrily, "You idiot! Call your zupervisor over, I vant to speak to somevone viz more intelligence!"

"Sorry," responds the officer, "he can'ta come. He'sa busy with a 2 guys in a Fiat Uno."

• • •

Air disaster in Ireland

Ireland's worst air disaster occurred yesterday when a small two-seater Cessna plane crashed into a cemetery early in the afternoon outside Limerick. Local search and rescue workers have recovered 300 bodies so far and expect that number to climb as digging continues.

• • •

Time is what keeps everything from happening at once.

Irish hunters

A couple of Irish hunters are out in the woods when one of them falls to the ground. He doesn't seem to be breathing; his eyes are rolled back in his head. The other guy whips out his mobile phone and calls 911. He gasps to the operator, "My friend is dead! What can I do?"

The operator, in a calm, soothing voice says, "Just take it easy, I can help. First, lets make sure he's dead."

There's silence, then the sound of a shot.

The hunter says, "OK, now what?"

• • •

Piet has been drinking all night, and when the barman calls "Time", he stands up to leave ... and falls flat on his face. So he pulls himself to his feet ... and falls over again. He thinks maybe he needs fresh air, so he drags himself out into the street, struggles to his feet ... and falls over. He decides to crawl the four blocks to his home, where he uses the doorhandle to pull himself up, opens the door ... and falls over. He crawls through the house, into his bedroom and tries one last time to stand up. He gets upright again but then collapses on to the bed, and is instantly asleep. He wakes up the next morning to find his wife standing over him shouting: "You were drunk again last night, weren't you?"

"What makes you say that?" asks Piet innocently. "The pub called. You left your wheelchair there again."

• • •

Paprika measure

2 dashes = 1 smidgeon
2 smidgeons = 1 pinch
3 pinches = 1 soupcon
2 soupcons = too much paprika

– Quoted by Martin Levin in "Phoenix Nest"

• • •

FBI top 10 deaths of the year

Every year the FBI is asked to investigate over 36 000 serious crimes including suspicious deaths and homicides. The Homicide Investigations Unit publishes its top homicides of the year. Here are 10 of them:

1. Debby Mills-Newbroughton, 99 years old, was killed as she crossed the road. She was to turn 100 the next day, but as she crossed the road with her daughter to go to her own birthday party, her wheelchair was hit by the truck delivering her birthday cake.

2. Peter Stone, 42 years old, is murdered by his 8-year-old daughter, who he had just sent to her room with no dinner. Young Samantha Stone felt that if she couldn't have dinner no one should, and she promptly inserted 72 rat poison tablets into her father's coffee as he prepared dinner. The victim took one sip and promptly collapsed. Samantha Stone was given a suspended sentence as the judge felt she didn't realise what she was doing, until she tried to poison her mother using the same method one month later.

3. David Danil, 17 years old, was killed by his girlfriend, Charla, after he attempted to have his way with her. His unwelcome advance was met with a double-barrelled shotgun. Charla's father had given it to her an hour before the date started, just in case.

4. Javier Halos, 27 years old, was killed by his landlord for failing to pay his rent for 8 years. The landlord, Kirk Weston, clubbed the victim to death with a toilet seat after he realised just how long it had been since Mr Halos paid his rent.

5. Megan Fry, 44 years old, was killed by 14 state troopers after she wandered onto a live-firing, fake-town, simulation. Seeing all the troopers walking slowly down the street, Megan Fry had jumped out in front of them and yelled "Boo!" The troopers, thinking she was a pop up target, fired 67 shots between them, over 40 of them hitting the target. She just looked like a very real-looking target, one of the troopers stated in his report.

6. Julia Smeeth, 20 years old, was killed by her brother Michael because she talked on the phone too long. Michael clubbed his sister to death with a cordless phone, then stabbed her several times with the broken aerial.

7. Helena Simms, wife of the famous American nuclear scientist Harold Simms, was killed by her husband after she had an affair with the neighbour. Over a period of 3 months Harold substituted Helena's eye shadow with a Uranium composite that was highly radioactive, until she died of radiation poisoning. Although she suffered many symptoms, including total hair loss, skin welts, blindness, extreme nausea and even had an ear lobe drop off, the victim never attended a doctor's surgery or hospital for a check up.

8. Military Sergeant John Joe Winter killed his two-timing wife by loading her car with Tri-nitrate explosive (similar to C4). The Ford Taurus she was driving was filled with 750 kilograms of explosive, forming a force twice as powerful as the Oklahoma bombing. The explosion was heard by several persons, some up to 14 kilometres away. No traces of the car or the victim were ever found, only a 55-metre deep crater, and 500 metres of missing road.

9. Patty Winter, 35 years old, was killed by her neighbour in the early hours of a Sunday morning. Her neighbour, Falt Hame, for years had a mounted F4 phantom jet engine in his rear yard. He would fire the jet engine, aimed at an empty block at the back of his property. Patty Winter would constantly complain to the local sheriff's officers about the noise and the potential risk of fire. Mr Hame was served with a notice to remove the engine immediately. Not liking this he invited Miss Winter over for a cup of coffee and a chat about the whole situation. What Winter didn't know was that he had changed the position of the engine. As she walked into the yard he activated it, hitting her with a blast of 5 000 degrees, killing her instantly, and forever burning her outline into the driveway.

10. Conrad Middleton, 26 years old, was killed by his twin brother Brian after a disagreement over who should take the family home after their parents passed away. Conrad had a nasal problem, and had no sense of smell. After the argument Brian stormed out of the house, then came back later and turned on the 3 gas taps in the house, filling it with gas. He then left out a box of cigars, a lighter and a note saying, "Sorry for the spree, have a puff on me, Brian". Conrad promptly lit a cigar, destroying the house and himself in the process.

• • •

The cheaper of two evils

Two recent court cases have earned the attention of newspaper readers in South Africa. One person was fined R1 000 for not having a TV licence. Another was released on bail of R500 after being arrested for murder. The moral of this South African story: if you do not have a TV licence and the inspector comes round, kill him. You'll save R500.

• • •

Apparently, 1 in 5 people in the world are Chinese. There are 5 people in my family, so it must be one of them. It's either my mum or my dad. Or my older brother Colin. Or my younger brother Ho-Cha-Chu.

But I think it's Colin.

• • •

Where do you find a dog with no legs?
Right where you left him.

• • •

If quitters never win, and winners never quit, what fool
came up with, "Quit while you're ahead"?

• • •

• • •

An atheist was taking a walk through the woods, admiring all that the 'accident of evolution' had created. "What majestic trees! What powerful rivers! What beautiful animals!" he said to himself.

As he was walking alongside the river, he heard a rustling in the bushes behind him. He turned to look. A 7-foot grizzly was charging towards him. He ran as fast as he could up the path. He looked over his shoulder and saw that the bear was closing.

He ran even faster, so scared that tears were coming to his eyes.

He looked over his shoulder again, and the bear was even closer. His heart was pumping frantically and he tried to run even faster.

He tripped and fell to the ground. He rolled over to pick himself up but saw the bear right on top of him, reaching for him with his left paw and raising his right paw to strike him.

At that instant the Atheist cried out "Oh Lord!"

Time stopped.

The bear froze.

The forest was silent.

Even the river stopped moving.

As a bright light shone upon the man, a voice came out of the sky, "You deny my existence for all of these years; teach others I don't exist; and even credit creation to a cosmic accident. Do you expect me to help you out of this predicament? Am I to count you as a believer?"

The atheist looked directly into the light. "It would be hypocritical to ask to be a Christian after all these years, but perhaps you could make the bear a Christian?"

"Very well," said the voice.

The light went out.

The river ran again.

And the sounds of the forest resumed.

And then the bear dropped his right paw ... brought both paws together ... bowed his head and spoke:

"Lord, for this food which I am about to receive, I am truly thankful."

• • •

Dear Abby

I am a sailor in the South African Navy.

My parents live in the suburb Woodstock and one of my sisters, who lives in Paarl North, is married to an Australian. My father and mother have recently been arrested for growing and selling marijuana and are currently dependent on my two sisters, who are prostitutes in Green Point. I have two brothers, one who is currently serving a non-parole life sentence in Pollsmoor Prison, Cape Town, for the rape and murder of a teenage girl in 1994; the other is currently being held in the Bellville remand centre on charges of incest with his three children. I have recently become engaged to marry a former Thai prostitute who lives in Sea Point and indeed is still a part time 'working girl' in a brothel; however, her time there is limited as she has recently been infected with an STD. We intend to marry as soon as possible and are currently looking into the possibility of opening our own brothel with my fiancée utilising her knowledge of the industry working as the manager. I am hoping my two sisters would be interested in joining our team. Although I would prefer them not to prostitute themselves, it would at least get them off the streets and hopefully the heroin.

My problem is this:

I love my fiancée and look forward to bringing her into the family and of course I want to be totally honest with her.

Should I tell her about my brother-in-law being an Australian?

• • •

Foregone conclusion

The Japanese eat very little fat and suffer fewer heart attacks than the British or Americans. On the other hand, the French eat a lot of fat and also suffer fewer heart attacks than the British or Americans. The Chinese drink very little red wine and suffer fewer heart attacks than the British or Americans. The Italians drink excessive amounts of red wine and also suffer fewer heart attacks than the British or Americans. Conclusion: Eat and drink what you like. It's speaking English that kills you.

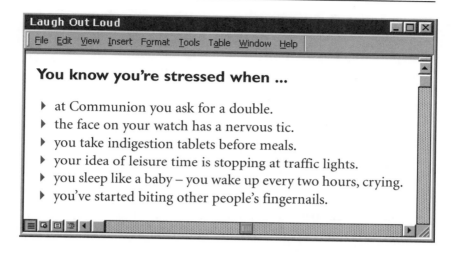

You know you're stressed when ...

▶ at Communion you ask for a double.
▶ the face on your watch has a nervous tic.
▶ you take indigestion tablets before meals.
▶ your idea of leisure time is stopping at traffic lights.
▶ you sleep like a baby – you wake up every two hours, crying.
▶ you've started biting other people's fingernails.

• • •

On life ... and death!

Eat right, exercise daily, live clean, die anyway.

Good health is merely the slowest possible rate
at which one can die.

Time is the best teacher ... unfortunately it kills all its students.

Despite the high cost of living, have you noticed how
it remains so popular?

• • •

SIGN IN A CAFETERIA:
Shoes are required to eat in the cafeteria.
Socks can eat anywhere they want.

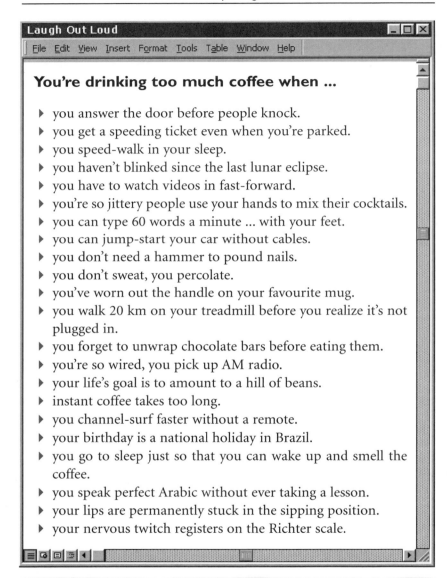

Laugh Out Loud ▭ □ ☒

File Edit View Insert Format Tools Table Window Help

You're drinking too much coffee when ...

▸ you answer the door before people knock.
▸ you get a speeding ticket even when you're parked.
▸ you speed-walk in your sleep.
▸ you haven't blinked since the last lunar eclipse.
▸ you have to watch videos in fast-forward.
▸ you're so jittery people use your hands to mix their cocktails.
▸ you can type 60 words a minute ... with your feet.
▸ you can jump-start your car without cables.
▸ you don't need a hammer to pound nails.
▸ you don't sweat, you percolate.
▸ you've worn out the handle on your favourite mug.
▸ you walk 20 km on your treadmill before you realize it's not plugged in.
▸ you forget to unwrap chocolate bars before eating them.
▸ you're so wired, you pick up AM radio.
▸ your life's goal is to amount to a hill of beans.
▸ instant coffee takes too long.
▸ you channel-surf faster without a remote.
▸ your birthday is a national holiday in Brazil.
▸ you go to sleep just so that you can wake up and smell the coffee.
▸ you speak perfect Arabic without ever taking a lesson.
▸ your lips are permanently stuck in the sipping position.
▸ your nervous twitch registers on the Richter scale.

*It might look like I'm doing nothing ...
but at the cellular level I'm really quite busy.*

Things you'd love to say but don't

- I refuse to enter a battle of the wits with you – it's against my morals to attack an unarmed person.
- We've been friends for a very long time – how about we call it quits?
- Congratulations on your new bundle of joy. Did you ever find out who the father was?
- Do they ever shut up on your planet?
- It sounds like English, but I can't understand a word you're saying.
- How about "never"? Is "never" good for you?
- You are such a good friend that if we were on a sinking ship and there was only one life jacket ... I'd miss you heaps and think of you often.
- I see you've set aside this special time to humiliate yourself in public.
- Let me show you how the guards used to do it.
- Whatever kind of look you were going for, you missed.
- Any connection between your reality and mine is purely coincidental.
- Don't bother me. I'm living happily ever after.
- Earth is full. Go home.
- Someday we'll look back on this, laugh nervously, and change the subject.
- If things get any worse, I'll have to ask you to stop helping me.
- If I want your opinion, I'll ask you to fill out the necessary forms.
- I will always cherish the initial misconceptions I had about you.
- I don't know what your problem is, but I'll bet it's hard to pronounce.
- I like you. You remind me of when I was young and stupid.
- Yes, I am an agent of Satan, but my duties are largely ceremonial.
- You sound reasonable ... time to up my medication.
- I'll try being nicer if you'll try being smarter.
- I'm out of my mind, but feel free to leave a message.

• • •

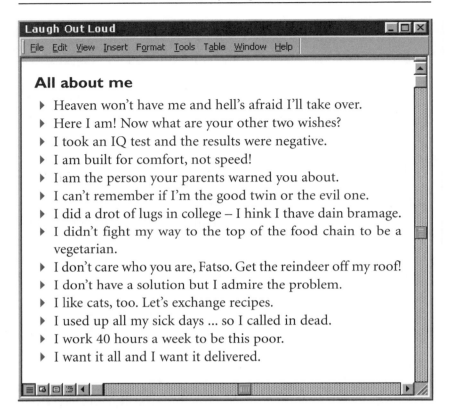

Laugh Out Loud ⬓ ⬜ ✕

File Edit View Insert Format Tools Table Window Help

All about me

▸ Heaven won't have me and hell's afraid I'll take over.
▸ Here I am! Now what are your other two wishes?
▸ I took an IQ test and the results were negative.
▸ I am built for comfort, not speed!
▸ I am the person your parents warned you about.
▸ I can't remember if I'm the good twin or the evil one.
▸ I did a drot of lugs in college – I hink I thave dain bramage.
▸ I didn't fight my way to the top of the food chain to be a vegetarian.
▸ I don't care who you are, Fatso. Get the reindeer off my roof!
▸ I don't have a solution but I admire the problem.
▸ I like cats, too. Let's exchange recipes.
▸ I used up all my sick days ... so I called in dead.
▸ I work 40 hours a week to be this poor.
▸ I want it all and I want it delivered.

• • •

Dear Abby
A couple of women moved in across the hall from me. One is a middle-aged gym teacher and the other is a social worker in her mid-twenties. These two women go everywhere together and I've never seen a man go into or leave their apartment. Do you think they could be Lebanese?

Dear Abby
What can I do about all the sex, nudity, language and violence on my VCR?

Dear Abby

I have a man I can never trust. He cheats so much, I'm not even sure the baby I'm carrying is his.

· · ·

Ever wonder ...

▸ why the sun lightens our hair, but darkens our skin?

▸ why a woman can't put on mascara with her mouth closed?

▸ why you never see the headline "Psychic Wins Lottery"?

▸ why 'abbreviated' is such a long word?

▸ why doctors call what they do 'practice'?

▸ why lemon juice is made with artificial flavour, while dishwashing liquid is made with real lemons?

▸ why the man who invests all your money is called a broker?

▸ why there isn't mouse-flavoured cat food?

▸ why Noah didn't swat those two mosquitoes?

▸ why they sterilize the needle for lethal injections?

▸ why they don't make the whole plane out of the material used for the indestructible black box?

▸ why sheep don't shrink when it rains?

▸ why they are called apartments when they are all stuck together?

▸ why con is the opposite of pro, but congress is not the opposite of progress?

· · ·

One good thing about repeating your mistakes is that you know when to cringe.

Dyslexics of the world, untie!

Look out for #1. Don't step in #2 either.

> My friend drowned in a bowl of muesli ...
> a strong currant pulled him in.

South African drivers

How to detect where the person driving next to you comes from ...

▸ One hand on wheel, one hand on hooter: PRETORIA

▸ One hand on wheel, one finger out window, banging head on steering wheel while stuck in traffic: DURBAN

▸ One hand on wheel, one finger out window, brick on accelerator, cutting across all lanes of traffic: SOWETO

▸ One hand on wheel, cell phone in other hand, newspaper across steering wheel, foot solidly on accelerator, gun in lap: JO'BURG

▸ One hand on wheel, one hand on 2-litre double-shot espresso: SANDTON

▸ One hand on non-fat double decaffeinated latte with cinnamon sprinkles, cell phone in other hand, one knee on wheel, driving up one-way street the wrong way: CAPE TOWN

▸ Both hands on wheel, both eyes shut, both feet above brake, quivering in terror: CAPETONIAN driving in JO'BURG

▸ One hand on wheel, Lion lager in other hand, dice hanging from rear-view mirror, throwing McDonald's bag out of the window: BENONI

▸ Four-wheel drive bakkie, semi-automatic shotgun mounted in rear window (with ammo belt), 'Klippies' bottle on floor, naartjie on antenna: VENTERSDORP

• • •

The young monk

A new young monk arrives at the monastery. He is assigned to help the other monks in copying the old canons and laws of the church by hand.

He notices, however, that all of the monks are copying from copies, not from the original manuscript. So the new monk goes to the head abbot to question this, pointing out that, if someone made even a small error in the first copy, it would never be picked up. In fact, that error would be continued in all of the subsequent copies.

The head monk says, "We have been copying from the copies for centuries, but you make a good point, my son."

So, he goes down into the dark caves underneath the monastery where the original manuscript is held in a locked vault that hasn't been opened for hundreds of years.

Hours go by and nobody sees the old abbot.

The young monk gets worried and goes downstairs to look for him. He sees him banging his head against the wall. His forehead is all bloody and bruised and he is crying uncontrollably.

The young man asks the old abbot, "What's wrong, father?"

With a choking voice, the old abbot replies, "The word is *celebrate*."

•••

Other ways of describing the not-so-smart

▶ A few clowns short of a circus
▶ A few fries short of a Happy Meal
▶ All foam, no beer
▶ Body by Fisher, brains by Mattel
▶ Warning: Objects in mirror are dumber than they appear
▶ He fell out of the stupid tree and hit every branch on the way down
▶ Doesn't have all his dogs on one leash
▶ One fruit loop shy of a full bowl
▶ Her antenna doesn't pick up all the channels

- Proof that evolution CAN go in reverse
- The receiver is off the hook
- Too much yardage between the goal posts

• • •

Learn Korean in 5 minutes (must be read out loud).

1. That's not right	Sum Ting Wong
2. Are you harbouring a fugitive?	Hu Yu Hai Ding?
3. See me ASAP	Kum Hia
4. Stupid Man	Dum Gai
5. Small Horse	Tai Ni Po Ni
6. Did you go to the beach?	Wai Yu So Tan?
7. I bumped the coffee table	Ai Bang Mai Ni
8. I think you need a facelift	Chin Tu Fat
9. It's very dark in here	Wao So Dim
10. I thought you were on a diet?	Wai Yu Mun Ching?
11. This is a tow-away zone	No Pah King
12. Our meeting is scheduled for next week	Wai Yu Kum Nao
13. Staying out of sight	Lei Ying Lo
14. He's cleaning his automobile	Wa Shing Ka
15. Your body odour is offensive	Yu Stin Ki Pu

• • •

Notice: all employees

Operations are now banned. As long as you are an employee here, you need all your organs. You should not consider having anything removed. We hired you intact. To have something removed constitutes a breach of employment.

• • •

The sign

Stupid people should have to wear signs that say, "I'm stupid." That way you wouldn't rely on them, would you? You wouldn't ask them anything. It would be like, "Excuse me ... oops, never mind. Didn't see your sign."

It's like when my wife and I moved. Our house was full of boxes and there was a removal truck in our driveway. My neighbour came over and said, "Hey, you moving?" "Nope. We just pack our stuff up once or twice a week to see how many boxes it takes."

A couple of months ago I went fishing with a mate of mine. We pulled his boat onto the ramp, I lifted up this big fish, and this idiot on the ramp goes, "Hey, did you catch that fish?" "No, I talked it into giving up."

Last time I had a flat tyre, I pulled my car into a petrol station. The attendant walked out, looked at my car, looked at me, and said, "Did your tyre go flat?" I couldn't resist. I said, "Nope. I was driving around and those other three just inflated themselves."

I was watching an animal show on the Discovery Channel. A guy invented a shark bite suit, and there was only one way to test it. "All right, Jimmy, you got that shark suit on. It looks good. They want you to jump into this pool of sharks and tell us if it hurts when they bite you." "Well, all right, but hold my sign. I don't wanna lose it."

I learned to drive an 18-wheeler and I misjudged the height of a bridge. The truck got stuck and I couldn't get it out no matter how I tried. I radioed in for help and eventually a local cop showed up to take the report. He asked, "So ... is your truck stuck?" I couldn't help myself! I looked at him, looked back at the rig, and then back at him and said, "No ... I'm delivering a bridge."

I stayed late at work one night and a co-worker looked at me and said, "Are you still here?" I replied, "No. I left about 10 minutes ago."

•••

Horror story

This story happened in Soweto, and even though it sounds like an Alfred Hitchcock tale, it's real.

This guy is on the side of the road hitch-hiking on a very dark night and in the middle of a storm. The night is rolling in and no car goes by. The storm is so strong he can barely see in front of him.

Suddenly he sees a car come towards him and stop.

The guy, without thinking, gets in the car and closes the door, only to realize that there is nobody behind the wheel. The car starts rolling forward slowly. The guy looks at the road and sees a curve coming his way. Scared, he starts to pray, begging for his life. He's still in shock when, just before he hits the curve, a hand appears through the window and moves the wheel.

The guy, paralysed with terror, watches how the hand appears every time they get to a curve.

Gathering strength, he gets out of the car and runs to the nearest township. Wet and in shock, he goes to a bar and asks for two shots of tequila and starts telling everyone about the horrible experience he went through.

A silence envelopes them all when they realise the guy is crying and isn't drunk.

About half an hour later, two wet and weary men walk into the same bar and one says to the other, "Look, Mfwetu, that's the idiot that got into the car while we were pushing it."

• • •

When confronted by a difficult problem, you can solve it more easily by reducing it to the question, "How would the Lone Ranger handle this?"

• • •

"Doc, I can't stop singing *The Green, Green Grass of Home*."

"That sounds like Tom Jones syndrome."

"Is it common?"

"It's not unusual."

Christmas cake recipe

Give this one a try this Christmas!

Ingredients:

1 cup of water	lemon juice
1 tsp baking soda	4 large eggs
1 cup of sugar	nuts
1 tsp salt	1 bottle Vodka
1 cup of brown sugar	cups of dried fruit

Sample the vodka to check quality.
Take a large bowl, check the vodka again.
To be sure it is of the highest quality, pour one level cup and drink.
Repeat

Turn on the electric mixer.
Beat one cup of butter in a large fluffy bowl.
Add one teaspoon of sugar.
Beat again.

At this point it's best to make sure the vodka is shtill OK.
Try another cup ... just in case.
Turn off the mixerer.

Break 2 leggs and add to the bowl and chuck in the cup of dried fruit.
Pick fruit off floor.
Mix on the turner.
If the fried druit gets stuck in the beaterers pry it loose with a drewscriver.

Sample the vodka to check for tonsisticity.

Next, sift two cups of salt. Or something.

Check the vodka.

Now shift the lemon juice and strain your nuts.

Add one table.

Add a spoon of sugar, or somefink. Whatever you can find.

Greash the oven.

Turn the cake tin 360 degrees and try not to fall over.

Don't forget to beat off the turner.

Finally, throw the bowl through the window, finish the vodka and kick the cat.

CHERRY MISTMAS

– Lemn Sissay (www.canongate.net)

•••

A bizarre death

At the 1994 annual awards dinner given for Forensic Science, the president, Dr Don Harper Mills, astounded his audience with the legal complications of a bizarre death. Here is the story:

On March 23, 1994, the medical examiner viewed the body of Ronald Opus and concluded that he died from a shotgun wound to the head. The decedent had jumped from the top of a ten-storey building intending to commit suicide. He left a note to that effect indicating his despondency. As he fell past the ninth floor, his life was interrupted by a shotgun blast passing through a window, which killed him instantly. Neither the shooter nor the decedent was aware that a safety net had been installed just below at the eighth floor level to protect some building workers and that Ronald Opus would not have been able to complete his suicide the way he had planned.

"Ordinarily," Dr Mills continued, "a person who sets out to commit suicide and ultimately succeeds, even though the mechanism might not be what he intended" is still defined as committing suicide. That Mr Opus was shot on the way to certain death nine stories below at street level, but that his suicide attempt probably would not have been successful because of the safety net, caused the medical examiner to feel that he had a homicide on his hands.

The room on the ninth floor from where the shotgun blast emanated was occupied by an elderly man and his wife. They were arguing vigorously, and he was threatening her with a shotgun. The man was so upset that, when he pulled the trigger, he completely missed his wife and the pellets went through the window striking Mr Opus. When one intends to kill subject A, but kills subject B in the attempt, one is guilty of the murder of subject B. When confronted with the murder charge, the old man and his wife were both adamant. They both said they thought the shotgun was unloaded. The old man said it was his long-standing habit to threaten his wife with the unloaded shotgun. He had no intention to murder her. Therefore, the killing of Mr Opus appeared to be an accident, that is, the gun had been accidentally loaded.

The continuing investigation turned up a witness who saw the old couple's son loading the shotgun about six weeks prior to the fatal accident. It transpired that the old lady had cut off her son's financial support and the son, knowing the propensity of his father to use the shotgun threateningly, loaded the gun with the expectation that his father would shoot his mother.

The case now becomes one of murder on the part of the son for the death of Ronald Opus. Now comes the exquisite twist. Further investigation revealed that the son was in fact Ronald Opus. He had become increasingly despondent over the failure of his attempt to engineer his mother's murder. This led him to jump off the ten-storey building on March 23rd, only to be killed by a shotgun blast passing through the ninth storey window. The son had actually murdered himself so the medical examiner closed the case as a suicide. Very tidy of him.

– Kurt Westervelt, *Associated Press*

Upon the advice of my attorney, my shirt bears no message at this time.

Favourite bumper stickers

▶ Forget about world peace ... visualise using your indicator.

▶ My karma ran over your dogma.

▶ Save a tree. Eat a beaver.

▶ Cover me. I'm changing lanes.

▶ I'm not driving fast – just flying low.

▶ Just give me chocolate and nobody gets hurt.

▶ I'm not as think as you drunk I am.

▶ I'm not tense, just terribly, terribly alert.

▶ Just what part of "NO" didn't you understand?

▶ So many pedestrians, so little time.

• • •

You know you're driving in South Africa when ...

▶ the road narrows and the guy to the rear of you has right of way.

▶ there is more space between the sole of your foot and the accelerator pedal than between your rear bumper and the car behind you.

▶ a solid white line in the middle of the road means "You MUST pass the car in front of you NOW."

▶ people stop at green lights and race through red ones.

▶ the driver in front of you tests his new ABS brakes.

▶ the driver behind you doesn't have ABS brakes.

• • •

A bus station is where a bus stops. A train station is where a train stops. On my desk, I have a work station ...

The Texas chili cook-off

Notes from an inexperienced chili taster named Frank:

"Recently I was honoured to be selected as an Outstanding Famous Celebrity in Texas, to be a judge at a chili cook-off because no one else wanted to do it. Also, the original person called in sick at the last moment and I happened to be standing there at the judge's table asking directions to the beer wagon when the call came. I was assured by the other two judges that the chili wouldn't be all that spicy and besides, they told me, I could have free beer during the tasting, so I accepted this as being one of those burdens you endure when you're an internet writer and therefore known and adored by all."

Here are the scorecards from the event:

▶ Chili # 1: Mike's Maniac Mobster Monster Chili

JUDGE ONE: A little too heavy on tomato. Amusing kick.
JUDGE TWO: Nice, smooth tomato flavour. Very mild.
FRANK: Holy smokes, what is this stuff? You could remove dried paint from your driveway with it. Took me two beers to put the flames out. Hope that's the worst one. These people are crazy.

▶ Chili # 2: Arthur's Afterburner Chili

JUDGE ONE: Smoky (barbecue?) with a hint of pork. Slight Jalapeno tang.
JUDGE TWO: Exciting BBQ flavour. Needs more peppers to be taken seriously.
FRANK: Keep this out of reach of children! I'm not sure what I am supposed to taste besides pain. I had to wave off two people who wanted to give me the Heimlich manoeuver. Shoved my way to the front of the beer line. The barmaid looks like a professional wrestler after a bad night. She was so irritated over my gagging sounds that the snake tattoo under her eye started to twitch. She has arms like Popeye and a face like Winston Churchill. I will NOT pick a fight with her.

▶ Chili # 3: Fred's Famous Burn-Down-the-Barn Chili

JUDGE ONE: Excellent firehouse chili! Great kick. Needs more beans.
JUDGE TWO: A beanless chili; a bit salty; good use of red peppers.
FRANK: This has got to be a joke. Call the EPA, I've located a uranium spill. My nose feels like I have been sneezing Drano. Everyone knows the routine by now and got out of my way so I could make it to the beer wagon. Barmaid pounded me on the back; now my backbone is in the front part of my chest. She said her friends call her "Sally". Probably behind her back they call her "Forklift".

▶ Chili # 4: Bubba's Black Magic

JUDGE ONE: Black bean chili with almost no spice. Disappointing.
JUDGE TWO: Hint of lime in the black beans. Good side dish for fish or other mild foods, not much of a chili.
FRANK: I felt something scraping across my tongue but was unable to taste it. Sally was standing behind me with fresh refills so I wouldn't have to dash over to see her. When she winked at me, her snake sort of coiled and uncoiled ... it's kinda cute.

▶ Chili # 5: Linda's Legal Lip Remover

JUDGE ONE: Meaty, strong chili. Cayenne peppers freshly ground adding considerable kick. Very impressive.
JUDGE TWO: Chili using shredded beef; could use more tomato. Must admit the cayenne peppers make a strong statement.
FRANK: My ears are ringing and I can no longer focus my eyes. I belched and four people in front of me needed paramedics. The contestant seemed hurt when I told her that her chili had given me brain damage. Sally saved my tongue by pouring beer directly on it from a pitcher. Sort of irritates me that one of the other judges asked me to stop screaming.

▶ Chili # 6: Vera's Very Vegetarian Variety

JUDGE ONE: Thin yet bold vegetarian variety chili. Good balance of spice and peppers.

JUDGE TWO: The best yet. Aggressive use of peppers, onions, and garlic. Superb.

FRANK: My intestines are now a straight pipe filled with gaseous flames. No one seems inclined to stand behind me except Sally. I asked if she wants to go dancing later.

▸ Chili # 7: Susan's Screaming Sensation Chili

JUDGE ONE: A mediocre chili with too much reliance on canned peppers.

JUDGE TWO: Ho Hum. Tastes as if the chef threw in canned chili peppers at the last moment. I should note that I am worried about Judge Number 3 – he appears to be in a bit of distress.

FRANK: You could put a hand grenade in my mouth and pull the pin and I wouldn't feel it. I've lost the sight in one eye and the world sounds like it is made of rushing water. My clothes are covered with chili which slid unnoticed out of my mouth at some point. Good, at the autopsy they'll know what killed me. Go Sally, save yourself before it's too late. Tell our children I'm sorry I was not there to conceive them. I've decided to stop breathing – it's too painful – and I'm not getting any oxygen anyway. If I need air, I'll just let it in through the hole in my stomach. Call the X-Files people and tell them I've found a super nova on my tongue.

▸ Chili # 8: Helen's Mount Saint Chili

JUDGE ONE: This final entry is a good, balanced chili, neither mild nor hot. Sorry to see that most of it was lost when Judge Number 3 fell and pulled the chili pot on top of himself.

JUDGE TWO: A perfect ending; this is a nice blend chili, safe for all, not too bold but spicy enough to declare its existence.

FRANK: Momma??!!

• • •

Light travels faster than sound. That's why some people
appear bright until they speak.

New meanings for US Government terrorism signs

These pictures, found on http://www.ready.gov as part of the US Government 'terrorism readiness' campaign, are so ambiguous they could mean anything! Here are a few interesting interpretations:

If you have set yourself on fire, do not run.

If you spot terrorism, blow your anti-terrorism whistle. If you are Vin Diesel, yell really loudly.

If you spot a terrorist arrow, pin it against the wall with your shoulder.

If you are sprayed with an unknown substance, stand and think about a cool design for a new tattoo.

Use your flashlight to lift the walls right off you!

The proper way to eliminate smallpox is to wash with soap, water and at least one (1) armless hand.

Hurricanes, animal corpses and your new tattoo have a lot in common. Think about it.

Be on the lookout for terrorists with pinkeye and leprosy. Also, they tend to rub their hands together manically.

If a door is closed, karate chop it open.

Try to absorb as much of the radiation as possible with your groin region. After 5 min 12 sec, however, you may become sterile.

 *After exposure to radiation, it is important to consider that you may have mutated to gigantic proportions: watch your head.*

 *If you hear the Backstreet Boys, Michael Bolton or Cliff Richard on the radio, cower in the corner or run like hell.*

 *If your lungs and stomach start talking, stand with your arms akimbo until they stop.*

 *If you are trapped, do not try to use flatulence to lift the debris.*

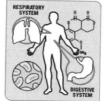 *If you lose a contact lens during a chemical attack, do not stop to look for it.*

 *Do not drive a station wagon if a power pole is protruding from the hood.*

 *A one-inch thick piece of plywood should be sufficient protection against radiation.*

 Always remember to carry food with you. At least you'll be able to enjoy a nice coke and apple while waiting to be rescued.

• • •

Take my advice – I don't use it anyway.

True bravery is to arrive home late after a boys' night out, wife waiting with broom, and you ask: "Are you still cleaning, or are you flying somewhere?"

24 fun things to do in an elevator

1. Grimace painfully while smacking your forehead and muttering, "Shut up, dammit, all of you just shut UP!"
2. Whistle the first seven notes of "It's a Small World" incessantly.
3. Crack open your briefcase or purse and, while peering inside, ask "Got enough air in there?"
4. Offer name tags to everyone getting into the elevator. Wear yours upside-down.
5. Stand silent and motionless in the corner, facing the wall, without getting off.
6. When arriving at your floor, grunt and strain to yank the doors open, then act embarrassed when they open by themselves.
7. Greet everyone getting into the elevator with a warm handshake and ask them to call you 'Admiral'.
8. On the highest floor, hold the door open and demand that it stay open until you hear the penny you dropped down the shaft go "plink" at the bottom.
9. Grin and stare at another passenger for a while, then announce, "I've got new socks on!"
10. When at least 8 people have boarded, moan from the back, "Oh, no, I'm gonna be sick!"
11. Meow occasionally.
12. Shout "Chutes away!" whenever the elevator descends.
13. Walk on with a cooler that says "human head" on the side.
14. Stare at another passenger for a while, then announce, "You're one of THEM!" and move to the far corner of the elevator.
15. Wear a hand puppet and talk to other passengers through it.
16. When the elevator is silent, look around and ask, "Is that your beeper?"
17. Say "Ding!" at each floor.
18. Ask "I wonder what all these do?" and push the red buttons.
19. Listen to the elevator walls with a stethoscope.
20. Draw a little square on the floor with chalk and announce to the other passengers that this is your 'personal space'.

21. Announce in a demonic voice: "I must find a more suitable host body."
22. Make explosion noises when anyone presses a button.
23. Wear X-Ray specs and leer suggestively at other passengers.
24. Stop at every floor, run off the elevator, then run back on.

• • •

Laugh Out Loud `_ □ ✕`

File Edit View Insert Format Tools Table Window Help

Eye exam

Count the number of F's in the following text – but don't cheat by reading further on:

> FINISHED FILES ARE THE RESULT OF YEARS OF
> SCIENTIFIC STUDY COMBINED WITH THE
> EXPERIENCE OF YEARS

How many did you count? Three? Wrong, there are six! Read again!

> FINISHED FILES ARE THE RESULT OF YEARS OF
> SCIENTIFIC STUDY COMBINED WITH THE
> EXPERIENCE OF YEARS

The reason is that the brain cannot process the word "OF". Anyone who counts all six F's on the first go is unusually observant. Three is normal.

• • •

Help Wanted: Telepath. You know where to apply.

Two attorneys have planned to meet for lunch, but one of them shows up 30 minutes late. The one who's been waiting asks his partner: "What kept you?"

"I ran over a Coke bottle and got a flat tyre."

"A Coke bottle in the road? Didn't you see it?"

"No, the kid had it under his coat."

•••

It's not hard to meet expenses, they're everywhere.

I can see clearly now, the brain is gone ...

Always glad to share my ignorance – I've got plenty.

•••

After a particularly poor game of golf, a popular club member skipped the clubhouse and started to go home. As he was walking to the parking lot to get his car, a policeman stopped him and asked, "Did you tee off on the sixteenth hole about twenty minutes ago?"

"Yes," the golfer responded.

"Did you happen to hook your ball so that it went over the trees and off the course?"

"Yes, I did. How did you know?" he asked.

"Well," said the policeman very seriously, "your ball flew out onto the highway and crashed through a driver's windshield. The car went out of control, crashing into five other cars and a fire truck. The fire truck couldn't make it to the fire, and the building burned down. So, what are you going to do about it?"

The golfer thought it over carefully and responded, "I think I'll close my stance a little bit, tighten my grip, and lower my right thumb."

•••

Changing light bulbs

How many members of the Impossible Missions Force does it take to change a light bulb?

FIVE: While Cinnamon creates a diversion by wearing a skimpy dress, I use a tiny narcotic dart to knock out the fascist dictator and remove his body. Rollin, wearing a plastic mask, masquerades as the dictator long enough for Barney to sneak up to the next floor, drill a hole down into the light fixture, remove the burned-out bulb, and replace it with a new super-high wattage model of his own design. Meanwhile, Willie has driven up to the door in a laundry truck. Just before Rollin's real identity is revealed, we escape to the laundry truck, drive to the airfield, and return to the United States.

How many existentialists does it take to screw in a light bulb?

TWO: One to screw it in and one to observe how the light bulb itself symbolises a single incandescent beacon of subjective reality in a netherworld of endless absurdity reaching out toward a cosmos of nothingness.

How many 'real men' does it take to change a light bulb?

NONE. 'Real Men' aren't afraid of the dark.

How many psychologists does it take to change a light bulb?

Just one ... if the bulb wants to change!

Variants:
1. Why should the light bulb HAVE to change? Why can't it be happy the way it is?
2. None. The light bulb will change itself when it's ready.
3. Just one, but it takes nine visits.

How many poets does it take to change a light bulb?

THREE. One to curse the darkness, one to light a candle, and one to change the bulb.

How many State engineers does it take to change a light bulb?

Avg. engineer = 130 pounds

Avg. engineer can lift ½ body weight over his head

$^{130}/_2$ = 65 pounds

Avg. light bulb = 4 oz. = .25 pounds

(1 Eng/65 pounds) x (.25 pounds) = 0.0038 engineers to change a bulb.

How many witches does it take to change a light bulb?

Into what?

How many stock brokers does it take to change a light bulb?

TWO. One to take out the bulb and drop it, and the other to try and sell it before it crashes.

How many university students does it take to screw in a light bulb?

TWO. One to hold the light bulb, and one to drink until the room spins.

• • •

What is a "free" gift? Aren't all gifts free?

Of all the things I've lost, I miss my mind the most.

With all the sadness and trauma going on in the world at the moment, it is worth reflecting on the death of a very important person, which went almost unnoticed last week. Larry La Prise, the man who wrote "The Hokey Pokey", died peacefully at home, aged 93. The most traumatic part for his family was getting him into the coffin ...

They put his left leg in ... and then the trouble started.

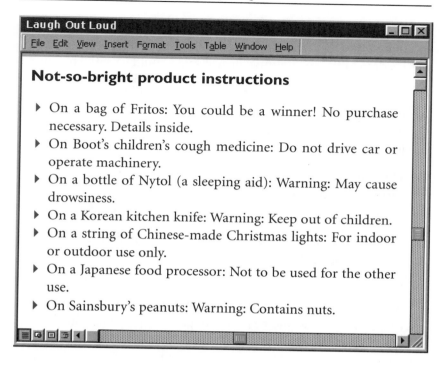

Laugh Out Loud

File Edit View Insert Format Tools Table Window Help

Not-so-bright product instructions

▸ On a bag of Fritos: You could be a winner! No purchase necessary. Details inside.

▸ On Boot's children's cough medicine: Do not drive car or operate machinery.

▸ On a bottle of Nytol (a sleeping aid): Warning: May cause drowsiness.

▸ On a Korean kitchen knife: Warning: Keep out of children.

▸ On a string of Chinese-made Christmas lights: For indoor or outdoor use only.

▸ On a Japanese food processor: Not to be used for the other use.

▸ On Sainsbury's peanuts: Warning: Contains nuts.

• • •

Courtroom questions

Q: Did he pick the dog up by the ears?
A: No.
Q: What was he doing with the dog's ears?
A: Picking them up in the air.
Q: Where was the dog at this time?
A: Attached to the ears.

Q: And lastly, Gary, all your responses must be oral. O.K.? What school do you go to?
A: Oral.
Q: How old are you?
A: Oral.

Q: Did you tell your lawyer that your husband had offered you indignities?

A: He didn't offer me nothing; he just said I could have the furniture.

Q: Could you see him from where you were standing?

A: I could see his head.

Q: And where was his head?

A: Just above his shoulders.

Q: The truth of the matter is that you were not an unbiased, objective witness, isn't it? You too were shot in the fracas?

A: No, sir. I was shot midway between the fracas and the naval.

Q: Doctor, how many autopsies have you performed on dead people?

A: All my autopsies have been on dead people.

Q: When he went, had you gone and had she, if she wanted to and were able, for the time being excluding all the restraints on her not to go, gone also, would he have brought you, meaning you and she, with him to the station?

MR. BROOKS: Objection. That question should be taken out and shot.

• • •

Times Media recently held its annual golf day, where one of the stories at the prizegiving highlighted the single-mindedness of golfers. A player arrived home one night, threw his clubs in the cupboard and sank exhausted into an armchair. His wife asked how the day had gone. "Remember Harry, who always partners me?" he replied. "He dropped dead on the 10th tee today. It was terrible."

"No wonder you look so exhauted," his wife commiserated.

"Too right," said the husband. "All the way around the back nine it was the same: hit the ball, drag Harry, hit the ball, drag Harry."

– From "Did you hear?" in the *Financial Mail*

• • •